chair out, knew wine and was able to drop that he flew private to Burning Man and had a surf cabin in Nosaro without seeming braggy.

"I know I should play it cool but I just want to say I had a great time." Later he pecked her on the cheek and held open the door of the private car he ordered her.

Doug was, as her sister had advertised, the full package and it bored her. Just thinking of him made her stifle a yawn as she walked down the hall of her Koreatown building that night. Turning a corner, she found a gangly homeless-looking man banging on the apartment door opposite hers. Apparently, his name was Spider and he was plant-sitting while her neighbors were in Iceland but had gotten too high and locked himself out. Amy found all this out as they were lying on the concrete floor of her apartment, not even able to make it to the couch before having sex.

"What!" her co-worker Yuri shouted when she got to that part of the story.

"Keep your voice down," she said. But heads were already jack-in-the-boxing up in their cube farm.

"So, a smart handsome CEO took you out for drinks and you went home and smooshed a homeless stranger on your apartment floor?"

"He's not homeless, he's plant-sitting."

"You're always saying you want something real." Yuri clucked his tongue. "Classic Amy."

"What is that supposed to mean?"

"Lemme guess. Amy ditched a nice guy for another emotionally unavailable bad boy." Fat Hank, a few cubes down, crab-walked his creaky chair towards them.

"Like the time she ditched Stewie in accounts for the bike messenger with crystal meth teeth?" It was Oola, her boss, joining the fray now. "Classic Amy."

"Classic Amy," they all murmured together like the refrain in a horror movie.

"Classic Amy," the new intern with glowing skin and an ass that had the mailroom boys buzzing agreed as she walked by sucking a boba tea.

"You just started Monday!" Amy shot up so fast her office chair toppled soundlessly onto the industrial carpet. "You don't get to 'Classic Amy'-me!"

The next date with Doug was, by anyone's account, a "10," and the following dates even better. He took her to an impossible-to-get-a-reservation-pop-up-yakitori in a refurbished grain elevator downtown; a reunion tour of a riot grrrl-type band she'd name-checked in passing; the fire-pit adorned patio of his new 'loft' apartment overlooking the arts district while saying all the right things about regretting being part of the gentrification process.

And yet each of those nights ended with her rolling around on her unswept apartment floor with Spider and his stale marijuana breath and uncut toenails, her phone blinking with one of Doug's thoughtful "Home safe?" texts.

Amy's therapist looked surprised to see her back that Tuesday as if nothing had happened.

"I thought we discussed this. That I couldn't be your therapist any—"

"Why am I attracted to the wrong men?" Before he could respond she blew through the story of Doug and Spider and the baby-faced intern with the peach of an ass parroting "Classic Amy."

"Can you just—like—help me for once?" she said, employing doe eyes and prayer hands. "And I don't mean talk about my childhood. For real—if you bring up my father again, I'll scream."

Dr. Ted steepled his soft fingers and sighed deeply.

"Well… I do have one last idea," he said.

He produced a shiny tablet from his desk, opened it wide and dimmed the lights. On the screen the actor Sir Patrick Stewart wore a blood red blazer, sitting by a fire with a brandy and reading a prop-sized book of Shakespeare's sonnets.

"What's happening? Is this porn?" Amy said. Dr. Ted shushed her.

Having found the camera, Sir Patrick was talking. "In this

4

age of infinite distractions do you ever wish your heart got a nudge in the right direction? Well, you're not alone. Extreme Emotional Dysfunction, or EED, affects one out of every 10 people. But now there's help for those of us who want to make better choices."

P-Stew held up a large red pill with a cupid's arrow graphic.

"Luckily Adorix™ is the world's first medication to focus the heart with the speed and precision of an arrow from Eros himself." Sir Patrick popped the pill and his eyes turned to pulsating cartoon graphic hearts.

"A love potion? So cheesy… Will my insurance pay?"

"It's in its clinical trial phase so you don't have to pay, but there are risks and lots of paperwork—" Dr. Ted cut himself off. "Just watch the video."

Sir Patrick was giving instructions to take the pill 10 minutes before rendezvousing with "your special person" and warned against intimate contact with any third parties in between to avoid erroneous bonding. Suddenly out in the world, Sir Patrick mugged for the camera sidestepping a mailman, a nun and a large German Shepard before kissing the cheek of an ethnically ambiguous every-woman checking the mailbox of her picket fenced house.

"Hold it," Amy said. "Am I supposed to believe Jean-Luc Picard is into that butterface?"

"Shhhh!"

"He would never. Patrick Stewart fucks."

"Now I don't pretend to understand the science here. But I do know even a classically trained thespian like me couldn't act lovestruck this well!" With a wink, Sir Patrick followed his new love, hand in hand, up a walkway into a picture-perfect house as a scroll of side effects sped past.

Dr. Ted eased the lights on and raised his eyebrows to acknowledge that yes, he knew her mind was no doubt completely blown.

"I'm sure you have many, many, many questions."

"Nah. I get it," she said. "Let's do this."

When Doug opened the door to his apartment that

night, Amy could still taste the chalky residue of the bitter pill. She surprised him with a "bonding" bear hug like Dr. Ted had instructed, taking in a nose full of pheromones and eye-stinging cologne. Over dinner, she stared wide-eyed like Doug was one of those 3D posters you need to scrutinize to spy a dolphin or a rainbow. Quiet and aloof, she was waiting for something to happen. She would've popped a second pill if Dr. Ted hadn't been so stingy. She had to sign a mountain of NDAs just to get one. She was so distracted she missed several cues to smile politely or say LOL at Doug's jokes and later spilled a drop of post dinner port on his beige chaise.

"What in the actual fuck?" Doug said. "Be careful please."

It was his first time raising his voice or dropping an F-bomb with her.

As they worked side by side, attacking the spot with fresh sponges and a battalion of cleaning products, Amy felt something stir inside her. It was barely a tingle; she imagined it like a sprout poking through cracked asphalt. Careful not to spill, she filled her mouth with port and made an executive decision to sleep with Doug as soon as the bottle was finished.

That week Amy let everyone know she was in love and, lest they think this was her usual pattern, followed up in the same boastful breath with "and he's a nice guy."

"Except for between the sheets." She gave this jokey addendum only to skeptics like her sister and the intern with the ass to die for. "Then he's not so nice. Ha, ha!"

Equally amazing was the lack of longing when Amy now passed her neighbor's door. Invariably the key in her lock would trigger a Pavlovian appearance by Spider, suddenly behind her having just made a pizza bagel or packed a bong or paused a Korean slasher film, inquiring if she wanted to eat, smoke or watch with him.

"I've got an early morning," she would say over her shoulder, imagining herself the star of her very own Adorix™ commercial.

"You feel the medication is helping then?" Dr. Ted asked and clicked his Adorix™ -logo'd pen to start writing. "You like

it?"

"Like it? I love it! I want to marry it!" She was so giddy she laughed at her own dad joke. "Little things about him I once found off-putting or basic, I now can't get enough of."

Dr. Ted rolled a couple fingers for her to continue.

"Like I don't mind that he hums or resorts to utensils halfway through a sandwich or mindlessly tugs on his scrotum when thinking. The way he farts in bed is endearing even when he tosses the comforter over my head and makes me smell it. If I wasn't head over heels, I probably wouldn't be too keen on him turning on porn while we have sex or insisting on silence when he watches golf all day Sundays. But it's him being vulnerable and showing me who he is, right? Same with the rough stuff, but who am I to sex shame?"

Dr. Ted nodded and scribbled copious notes. When Amy was done rattling off Doug's endearing quirks, she held her palms out for that session's pill like it was holy communion. Amy didn't want to jinx herself by not taking the pill, but she suspected that this was real.

So at her nephew's lavish 1st birthday when Gwen approached Amy in front of the oyster bar and told her maybe she should consider slowing her roll with Doug, Amy told her to eat a box of dicks loud enough for the party clown to distractedly pop his in-progress balloon walrus.

"Sanjay invested a lot of money in Doug's ridesharing for pets app but he keeps needing more and forgetting the name of his own company. Thinking something was funky, Sanjay hired a detective and turns out Doug isn't even his real name and he declared bankruptcy last year and has been married thrice. He may also be an arsonist with genital warts."

"I knew it," Amy said. "You're jealous."

"I don't think you know him as well as you think."

"I know him well enough to be engaged to him."

Gwen held her own hand with its enormous ring up to her mouth in both horror and a not so subtle dig.

"Well, engaged to be engaged. Tonight's our one-month anniversary. Speaking of which he probably has something

amazeballs planned. As opposed to this." Amy motioned dismissively to the yard brimming with amusement park rides and mixologists on mini-ponies. She piled high a cocktail napkin of oysters to slurp in traffic and made her exit towards the valet, vowing to never drive to the Westside again.

"And thank god his name's not really Doug!" she yelled over her shoulder.

But that night not only did Doug or whatever his name was not have anything planned for the two of them, he didn't return any of Amy's 28 calls. Around dinner she resorted to cold-texting his friends and family and posting social media updates: ""Don't panic but has anyone seen my fiancé, 'Doug?!'"

He finally called to say he'd left his phone at the gym.

"Also," he cleared his throat. "I feel like this relationship is like a dog that we both once loved but now it's lame and in pain and the most mature thing to do is take it behind the barn and strangle it."

She laughed. Doug's humor was so dry. Most women wouldn't get it. Not Gwen. Not that chipper intern with the sick body.

"That isn't what you do with a lame dog, but it's so cute you think that," she said. "Also, I love you unconditionally. You're my best friend."

"I don't think you're hearing me. It's over." He paused; no doubt full of emotion. Then Amy heard a crunch like a handful of mixed nuts in his mouth. He was snacking. "It's been real."

She begged, she pleaded, she screamed until she realized she was screaming into a dead line.

Suddenly, there was a pounding on the door. Amy imagined it was Doug revealing that it was all a joke as he fanned a couple tickets to Bali or Jeju Island out in his hand. But it was just Spider, brandishing an old screwdriver like a switchblade, wondering if she was being attacked.

"Are you sure you're ok? I made cinnamon toast. Want a foot rub?"

"Goddamnit Spider, stop harassing me!"

Amy was in too much of a rush to notice his wet eyes as

she wrenched the screwdriver from his hand and took off down the hall.

Amy showed up at Doug's apartment a little before midnight. She realized this was a faux pas, but so was forcing her way into Dr. Ted's condo earlier wielding Spider's screwdriver and demanding pills. She'd jabbed Dr. Ted once to get his attention and they had both seemed surprised by how little give his abdomen had. He'd been so scared and blubbery she didn't think she could ever respect him enough to be his patient again.

"Doug!" Amy banged on his door and pushed the bell for ten minutes even after he'd yelled for her to go away and that he was calling the police.

"Guess who's not wearing any panties," she shout-whispered back. "Open up!"

All she needed was a minute alone with him to slip him the medication, screwdriver pressed to his Adam's apple if needed. It would be an awkward ten minutes waiting for the Adorix™ to take effect but then smooth sailing.

By now neighbors were rubber-necking out ajar doors, venturing into the tasteful hall, pajama-clad arms akimbo.

"I told you I'm busy. You're really freaking us out right now!"

"Us? Are you...?" she screamed. "Are you in there with someone?!"

Silence ensued, broken only by the chalky grinding of Amy's back molars.

By the time Doug yelled back that it wasn't any of her business Amy was sprinting circles down the building's dizzying stairwell as responding police were riding up in the elevator. Minutes later Amy was scaling a back-alley fire escape, and began winding her way up floor after floor, each window a little jewel box diorama of domesticity—couples cuddled on the couch streaming mutually agreed upon content—that felt both mocking and invigorating.

Her panting breath had barely steamed Doug's picture window when she caught sight of him with his arm around a twig of a girl, gorgeous, half-dressed and with sex hair; they struck a perfect-pair pose to the police interviewing them at the

door. Amy felt confident she could destroy this girl's face forever with a few quick jabs.

"I love you Doug!" she screamed, banging madly on the locked window pane. Startled, the four of them looked over just in time to see Amy lose her balance and disappear.

Head throbbing, Amy woke up in a squeaky hospital bed. She was disappointed to find Dr. Ted and Gwen, not Doug, sitting by her side. A slim camera on a tripod sat opposite her and she didn't like the look of the armed guard standing in the doorway.

"Where's Doug?" she croaked and motioned for a glass of water.

"Jesus, Amy."

"You've been in a coma for three days."

Her sister buzzed for a nurse and Dr. Ted said he was texting the lawyers. He kept cringing and touching himself where she stabbed him.

Amy was dizzy and disoriented and seeing her sister and psychologist in the same room didn't help. It felt like a bad network crossover episode.

"I've been out three days?" Amy remembered the shock on Doug's face as he watched her slip from view.

"Luckily for you those garbage bags—" Gwen said.

"—Broke your fall," Dr. Ted concluded.

She didn't like the way they were finishing each other's sentences. Clearly, they'd been talking. She felt ganged up on and disappointed to see she wasn't hooked up to any self-administering meds. She fingered the bandage on the back of her head and caught the armed guard craning around to look at her.

"Anyone gonna tell me why there's an armed guard at the door?"

But they were both talking at her now. Droning on about how the police wanted to take her into custody but the pharmaceutical company had gotten involved, Dr. Ted needed six stitches, and she'd given them all quite a scare and made such a mess.

"Obviously I could press charges but Adorix™ prefers I don't." Dr. Ted scratched below his belly button. "I still could though, but I won't."

As they kept talking Amy looked around, noticing the room was dotted with flowers. There was a teddy bear in a white doctor's coat sitting on the bedside table. The bear's name tag read "Dr. Hugs." Classic Doug, she thought.

Dr. Ted was still talking about how he couldn't take hot baths until he got the stitches out. He loved a good hot bath.

"Maybe I should be the one to sue you. Your little wonder drug…." Amy hesitated. It was hard for her to point fingers at the miracle drug. "I think the dosage was too high."

"Amy…" he started to talk in an annoyed tone Amy hated.

"Amy…" Gwen said in the same tone.

"You waived your rights to sue anyone. More importantly the drug didn't make you do this, I'm sorry to say." Dr. Ted didn't look sorry. "It was a clinical trial. We were using a placebo."

Dr. Ted removed a red pill from his shirt pocket as a visual aid.

"What?"

"A placebo is a—"

"I know what a placebo is, Gwen!"

The shout echoed in the room, startling everyone, even the guard at the door. Gwen and Dr. Ted exchanged glances. Amy didn't care anymore if they had fucked while she was in a coma. She clenched the cold bed sheets to keep her hands from shaking.

"I think what happened here is you fell back into your behavior pattern." Dr. Ted almost seemed to be enjoying this. "Your routine."

"You mean when she goes after a man who's unattainable and bad for her?" Gwen piped in and wagged her head.

"That's insane!"

"Is it though?" It was like they were getting off on gaslighting her.

"First off, Doug isn't one of my usual bad boys." Amy felt on solid ground with this. "He's a nice guy."

"That's what we thought at first. But he's wanted in five

states for fraud. The detective even—"

"But—but—Look at all these flowers!"

Dr. Ted and Gwen both winced like Amy was a lame dog that needed to be strangled.

"Ant brought this stuff," Dr. Ted said quietly, then crinkled his brow. "Flea?"

"You mean Spider?"

"He seemed sweet," Gwen offered. "Poor and dirty, but sweet."

"But…" Amy felt her case weakening and doubled down. "Everything that happened was because of the pill."

"You mean the placebo."

"I mean the pill!"

"You mean your pattern."

"I didn't just do all that on my own." Amy hoped this whole exchange was some advanced phase of the clinical trial, like a test. "I don't pull screwdrivers on people. I don't scale apartment buildings."

"You did slash that guy's tires once," Gwen offered with the 'I'm sorry' face she made when throwing Amy under the bus. "And you can be pretty stalky."

"Amy there's no doubt that you went to unprecedented measures in pursuing Doug. The belief that you were really truly chemically indisputably 'in love' justified that. In your mind it gave you carte blanche for egregious behavior." Dr. Ted was really milking his moment.

"You were back on your old bullshit but on steroids," Gwen said just in case Amy wasn't getting the message loud and clear.

Amy wanted to protest but what was the point. Classic Amy. She sat there while Dr. Ted went on at length about how there would be an exit interview with a couple Adorix™ reps later that day. When Amy complained he said it was non-negotiable and exchanged a glance with the guard.

Seeing she had no fight left in her, Gwen went into the hall to track down a nurse. Looking like he didn't want to be alone with her, Dr. Ted said something about getting himself a snack from the vending machines and followed. Neither said anything about being glad she woke up from a coma.

Exhausted, Amy lay under the stale sheets in her thin hospital gown. Had she really managed to cast aside a good guy while in pursuit of another shitheel? She looked at the doctor teddy bear staring blankly at her and knocked it to the floor. When it fell, she noticed the red pill Dr. Ted had taken out sitting on the bedside table. The placebo. Maybe he left it behind in case she wanted to get it tested. No bother, she mostly believed him.

But still. In tears, she jammed the pill in her mouth and swallowed hard, gagging loud enough for the guard to glance back at her. As the bitter taste dissipated in her mouth, she pulled her knees to her chest and hugged herself tightly, breathing herself in and rocking back and forth, hoping to bond.

GOOD IN A ROOM

MY JOKES FALL FLAT.

I'm flailing in the room and have been for weeks, maybe months.

My one-liners are stepped on. My blows don't land and my tags are talked over. My asides drop from the side of my mouth, stillborn. My pitches sputter out as I'm met with angled heads and scrunched brows. And those are the rare spurts when I'm vocalizing. The bulk of the long days my mouth moves only to chew stale Costco gum. I stare at the story notes scrawled on the grease board like they were rocket science. I play mind games with the clock.

I used to be, what is known in the industry, as "good in the room." Some guys are great at breaking stories, others have a knack for delegating, there are the anti-social ones who churn out killer scripts, ones who can't write but excel at punching-up jokes. Fitzy always said a room was doomed to fail without a token fat guy who laughed a lot for good luck.

I'm the all-around utility man. "Meet Bruce," I imagine my agents pitching me to employers. "He's been around the block.

15

He's good in a room."
At least, I *was.*
Then Xander arrived. He replaced our previous assistant, Tonya, who left mid-season after getting an offer from a streaming service to develop a limited series based on her social media feed. Or something like that. At least Tonya kept the fridge stocked with La Croix and treaded lightly.

His very first day I was telling a story over lunch to the room about the time one of the writers on *Funnier by the Dozen* put a big pink dildo in the water cooler. Don't ask me how Fitzy got it in there. What a lunatic! He used to drive to the office with a rubber sex doll in shotgun so he could use the HOV lane. Anyway, I was in the middle of the story when Xander walked by passing out scripts.
"That's so funny," he interrupted to say. *I'm in the middle of the story!*
I lost my place and totally flubbed the punchline (which has to do with the star of the show obliviously drinking from the cooler while we all watched horrified) and the story, which usually slays, finished limply with the writers smiling politely and checking their phones. Xander hummed along obviously.
The thing about working in a room is you have to know your place. Rooms run on energy and vibe and any little thing can throw the balance off. Idiosyncrasies and quirks (and who's quirkier than a roomful of writers) that are endearing on day one snowball into piercing annoyances after months on end of being sealed in a hermetic little blister of stale air-conditioning and coffee breath. Vocal frys, facial tics, sneezing fits, hyena laughs, throat-clearing, dandruff-dusting, too much cologne or not enough; it can all amplify into its own form of waterboarding. I remember years ago on *Pickles and Mr. D* a fist fight broke out because of the way a junior writer methodically peeled his string cheese.
But this Xander. The nagging issue is there is no *one specific thing* that burns my buns. Nothing I can jerk him aside and ask him to cut out or tone down or even for me to bring up to the showrunner without seeming nit-picky. It's a confluence of

countless little things—a thousand tiny paper cuts I find myself nursing as I drag myself out of the room and towards the car park every night, wondering what I'm gonna do for dinner.

It's his downcast eyes when he corrects me after I mispronounce "meme" in the room. His furrowed brow, agape mouth combo instead of laughter when—after someone mentions the upcoming Rockford Files reboot with a trans lead—I quip "What's next? Bi-curious Columbo?" leading me to then defensively explain my joke and the fact that I support diversity and representation 110%. It's the overly earnest way he said "that looks comfy" about the special blue plastic pillow I sit on for lumbar support.

On the surface, Xander's no different from any assistant in any room I've worked in. The eager beaver morning greetings, ironic t-shirts, deferential demeanor, the obscure pop culture references in lieu of jokes. If anything, I should have a soft spot for him. I'm pretty generous with my time mentoring 'baby' writers. For example, I took our junior staff writer, Kelly, to my favorite little hole in the wall Thai place for lunch the very first week and offered to give notes on her *Young Sheldon* spec script.

But Kelly knows her place. She would never make a point of saying she'd never heard of *Pickles and Mr. D* or make a comment about my phone's large font size or refer to my jeans as "retro." She would never say "that's funny!" as opposed to actually laughing at my jokes.

Then there's the donuts. The very first week he brings donuts for the room. Expensive donuts. *Fancy* donuts.

There's a reason the breakroom is stocked with dry granola bars and gaudy cans of flavored water. We're too busy with long hours, hellish commutes and family whatever to make it to the gym or even reach our step-count; so fancy donuts aren't helping the situation. I'm pretty sure Malika is diabetic. And I'll be the first to admit I've put more than a few pounds on since I've had to start fending for myself at home.

Of course, the room cooed and thanked him but we all resented the gesture. I downed a coconut and half a sprinkle thing and spent the rest of day distracted, wanting to reach

into the pink box for the other half. Xander ate a jumbo jelly—standing there licking his fingers cartoonishly and modeling his narrow little waist for us. At that age you can eat anything. His designer t-shirts and pants are tight enough to look tailored—he dresses like a little Gen Z action figure. Another thing is his face is covered in this downy peach fuzz. In the room it catches the fluorescents like mist or a halo or something. It's so distracting. I want to pin him to the floor and shear him down like a sheep.

Every Wednesday morning like clockwork he trots in another big pink rectangle of hipster donuts. *Humpday donuts* he calls them and even raps a little ditty about them, recording himself on his phone the whole time. We cram around the box, thanking him in one breath and scolding him for tempting us with carbs in the next. The lithe elf doesn't understand we're not being sarcastic. The thing about a room is, you have to be able to read it. But he's too busy humming to himself and looking thin and recommending this new band or that new TikTok account. Our showrunner compliments him for being on the "bleeding edge" but I just wish he could just make a decent pot of goddamn coffee!

Listen, I have zero issue with younger writers. I'm arguably middle-aged, not even the oldest writer in the room—Phil is way older, as evidenced by his hair dyed so black it gives off a purple hue when the midday sun hits it. I listen to Kanye, after all.

I mean Kelly doesn't get on my nerves. Yesterday we hoofed the extra few blocks at lunch to go to a favorite pho spot of mine. We had plenty to talk about.

She said *Funnier by The Dozen* was, like, her favorite show. We talked so long we were 10 minutes late returning to the office and the writers had already started up again. We crept back into the room with sheepish shrugs and hurried to take our seats.

"Well nice of you two to grace us with your presence," Phil said in a school marm's falsetto, his back to us as he scrawled plot points on the grease board. "You two go to Vietnam for that pho or what?"

Kelly and I exchanged a conspiratorial glance across the table. It was just a nice moment.

Then I could swear Xander looked up from his keyboard to raise an eyebrow at me in mock reproach or like he's onto me or something. I spent the rest of the afternoon silently trying to figure out what the hell that was supposed to mean.

A common mistake for a writers' assistant is to chime in too much in the room. Their job is to type what we, the professional writers, say for us all to see on the big-screen monitor. Of course, it's not a dictatorship. The room initially laughed, me included, the first few times Xander chimed in. You want to be inclusive and help others learn the craft. But you give this kid an inch. Emboldened by our generosity, Xander's been firing off little wisecracks and bon mots all over the place. I wouldn't call them jokes, really. They're Twitter references and snarky asides really. I'm not saying they're all awful but they're not the tone of the show and so it's just a waste of all our time. Lately, he's so busy pitching his own "jokes" that a few of ours have gotten lost in the room's hubbub. Mine in particular.

Today we're punching-up a scene and I pitch out a fun line of dialogue.

"*Or better yet, let's forget this ever happened!*" I say.

I watch on the monitor as Xander rapidly types out Kelly's pitch, Malika's pitch, Joel's pitch, etc. In fairness, sometimes with so many writers yakking at once the assistant doesn't always catch everything.

"*Or better yet, let's forget this ever happened!*" I pitch again, this time punctuating the line with a little chuckle.

Still Xander doesn't type it out on the monitor and by now he's moved the cursor down the page to a clunky couplet between our star and his sleazy dentist.

"*Or better yet, let's forget this ever happened.*" I say it again. Then again, louder just so there can be no mistake. I practically scream it. By now everyone's looking down the table at me, including Xander.

"Forget *what* happened?" Xander asks innocently.

"What? That's the joke I'm pitching to you—"

"Oh! Right. My bad." Xander apologizes. He always apologizes.

My face is hot as Xander scrolls up to the previous scene and slowly types my pitch out, inserting it into the existing dialogue. Of course, with all the preceding drama, the joke has a lot riding on it...

And yet the line still manages to underwhelm my lowest expectations.

The line just lies there on the screen, funny as a ransom note. It's worse than a hack joke (we call them "clams") and may as well be a Mad Lib for all the sense it makes in the scene. It's gibberish.

The room sits there, reading it silently over and over like a mantra. No one says shit for an eternity.

"Maybe..." Phil says with as much diplomacy as he can muster, then pauses to chew the end of a pen with his capped teeth. "Maybe that line's not really working, Bruce."

"No worries, no worries," I'm quick to mumble.

"I'll save that joke for my memoir," I add, offering a go-to writers' room line for saving face that's neither original nor face-saving.

"Okey-dokey," Xander says, scrolling the cursor back down the page, but then adds quietly, "I'll guess we'll all just forget *that* ever happened. "

It's the lowest of low hanging fruit. Reiterating a variation on my own botched joke and using it against me is the lowest form of sitcom hack humor but since it comes from the unlikeliest of sources, the writers' assistant, it gets big laughs from the room. Like when the shortest guy on the basketball team scores.

It wasn't long ago that I wouldn't have missed a beat before firing a quiver full of my own retaliatory one-liners in his direction. I would've absolutely destroyed him and left the rest of the room giggling in the process. Fitzy and I used to entertain the room for hours going at each other.

Now, my mouth is dry and all I can think to do is offer a paternalistic tip of my imaginary hat in Xander's direction to show what a good sport I am. The lameness of my gesture is like gas on a fire, ratcheting up the hysterical laughing.

It's the kind of can't-catch-your breath hysterics that I

remember once being able to cause, instead of being the butt of. The laughing snowballs to that point where the laughter itself becomes its own self-propelling joke. My colleagues wipe their eyes and cast apologetic looks in my direction as they straighten up in an effort to get "back to business" only for their shoulders to shake and lips to quiver as they start wheezing with laughter again. Every time it sounds like it's finally dying out, another wave of giggles swells up and crashes around me.

I sit limply, sweat tearing down from my armpits and surfing the waves of my belly, pooling around my waistband. I don't dare move in my chair for fear of being audibly squishy. My face must be shiny and pink as a baboon's ass right now. No wonder they can't catch their breath—the pathetic sight of me impotently grinning and unable to sputter even a grade school comeback—is worth a thousand tickling fingers. I catch Kelly steal a sideways glance of pity at me like I'm road kill. Even she's giggling and panting too, her blonde bangs darkened with sweat. She shrugs helplessly in my direction. I forgive her though. Not him, but her. Fitzy used to say being good in a room means being a team player.

***

"Didn't you write on *Cheaper Than Therapy*?" Malika asks me through a mouthful of salad greens. Eager to spin war stories, I glance over from my tuna melt only to find her holding up that day's *Hollywood Reporter* folded back to display for me an old photo of Fitzy buried deep in the paper. My breath quickens. Guys of Fitzy's age don't make the trade papers with spec sales or show deals so I know right away. His cleaning lady found him on a lounger on the back patio overlooking his condo's common space. The piece didn't list the cause of death but I blamed it on the last room he worked in—a basic cable workplace comedy about a sexy yoga studio. Over happy hour whiskeys one night the previous spring, Fitzy said the twenty-something bosses called him into their office where they were playing video games and told him he just wasn't "jibing with the room." Two weeks later on his last day he got to pick where they ordered lunch from.

"My first show," I say to Malika and anyone else listening after reading the item and writing down the funeral info. "Fitzy

was hilarious. Kind of a mentor, really. One of the best scribes in the biz. Rest in peace."

Instead of launching into one of a dozen classic stories about him, I excuse myself to the bathroom, douse my face with water and wonder where I could bring my suit to get pressed before the funeral. When I return to the room, I don't mention the matter again. Same as when the dog died or my wife Sheila decamped for Wyoming. Being in a comedy room means leaving the drama at the door.

I'm sure Xander's never heard of *Cheaper Than Therapy* either.

It's not exactly storming the beaches at Normandy, but I am the last generation of Americans raised by television, collectively co-parented by a patchwork of Bradys, Bunkers, Partridges and Waltons. Mike Brady's perm, J.J's STD scare, Samantha the witch's new Darren; all shook me to my core. I'm the vestige of sitting lotus-style, back then we called it Indian, and brain-numbingly close to the glowing screen so as to more easily crank the channel. By hand! The last generation to fiddle with the antenna for reception. I remember holding the goddamn rabbit ears to keep the static at bay for hours so my older brothers could watch the Celtics. I'm the last generation, and this is the kicker, to twist that knob to find a measly four channels at my service. A few more if I spun the UHF knob. Around dinner time we got our news from one of the holy trinity of well-coiffed white guys: Jennings, Rather or Brokaw. And sometime after midnight the National Anthem blared followed by a blast of static or a Native American appeared on a test pattern screen to nudge us gently to bed.

I'm the last generation to watch something for no other reason than because it was, well... on. We all watched the same damn thing. Sewer systems exploded from coast to coast right after the series finale of *M*A*S*H* because 100 million people had waited for the credits to take a piss. It unified us as a country.

This was all before the culture fragmented, splintering like rotted wood into a million shards each with its own YouTube stars and subscription packages and is it any wonder why the

country feels so chewed up and spat out. Now we all just churn out a steady ooze of "content" in hopes that something raises eyebrows. I could tell things were bottoming out with Sheila when we couldn't decide on a show to watch together. Sheila, I still remember our first date to a live taping of Johnny Carson and then Benihana. I made her laugh so hard sake came out her nose. She loved that about me. Fucking Xander. What kind of name is that anyway. He's less a person than an algorithm combined of everything that's gone rotten in this business. I'm sure he has no idea that a character I co-created once had his own Burger King glass or that fast food franchises even used to give out actual glasses. I'm sure the kid has no idea who Alan fucking Alda is.

Fitzy's funeral is a low-key affair at a Catholic church that smells like mildew out in Tarzana. I jotted some things down on an index card in case anyone wants me to say a few words but it's hard to tell who's in charge. I spot his stepson, who's been in and out of rehab, sneaking a smoke outside and he tells me the service is just for friends and family to give remembrances. I nod dumbly only realizing when I sit down that's exactly *who I am*! I should've pressed harder. If my ex was here she would've known what to do. I wonder if Sheila knows about Fitzy.

Fitzy hated all religions and the church funeral is one last poke in the eye from his estranged wife. No one says much besides the slurring priest and what they do say is boilerplate niceties. His brother-in-law tells a fucking golf story. What's sadder than a writer's funeral peppered with clichés and banalities? Cheryl who played the horny neighbor on *Cheaper by the Dozen* is a few pews in front of me. She looks terrible but it's a nice gesture for her to come. I reintroduce myself to her at the reception at the daughter's cramped apartment a few miles away and she mutters my name four or five times before a smile of remembrance lights up her face, her veneers smeared with plum lipstick. She slips me a business card with a little headshot and outdated resume on the back.

"You were always very clever," she says, squeezing my arm with affection or to steady herself as she scans the room.

I keep waiting for there to be a little moment for us to make toasts or trade stories. Finally, the daughter gets up and thanks everyone for coming and points out that non-permitted parking on the street expires in a few minutes. Everyone starts hurrying out, mumbling they'll be right back but nobody returns. I linger for a minute, finishing my cheap white wine and watching Cheryl wrap a couple of deviled eggs in napkins and tuck them in her purse.

When I return home, I don't leave the apartment complex for the rest of the weekend. I mosey to check my mail every few hours hoping to exchange waves with a neighbor or two. But as usual everyone's vertical blinds are shut. Melrose Place it ain't. The dinky pool's been closed for repairs for months and the only resident who hangs in the common area is a pasty girl talking to her phone who waves me away to make sure I don't walk through her livestream or Tik Tok. I'm old enough to remember when people were famous for a reason, I want to yell.

Saturday morning, I squeeze a handful of limes to make a pitcher of fresh margaritas and settle into the couch just in time for the start of *Lonesome Dove* on cable. What a mini-series. I nurse a big bowl of popcorn doused with seasoning and console myself thinking I could never do this when Sheila was around for a variety of reasons the least of which being, she hated westerns. Ironic considering now she lives on a ranch in Wyoming with some carpetbagger she met on Match.com. Our daughter, forever in massage school in Portland living with a still married EMT, went there last Christmas for a whole week and I got her for two lousy days over Thanksgiving because, according to her, there's "nothing festive about the Valley." Her and her married boyfriend are the type of people that love to tell everyone they don't own a television. I'm pretty tanked and misting up by the time the doc tells Robert Duvall they need to amputate his other leg too.

I should've said something at the goddamn funeral.

I can't sleep and get up extra early on Monday and do some push-ups and sit-ups for the first time in years. I crank up Bob

Segar in the car and drive around for a while. I'm not even sure where I'm going and then I pass just the kind of over-priced donut shop I hate. They're everywhere now, I guess. I pull a U-turn.

I bring a big box of donuts—fancy ones—to the room. Everyone makes a big deal asking what's gotten into me and making jokes about me stealing Xander's thunder. I laugh it off, telling them I'm mixing it up a little bit and ain't that the truth. I chomp into a coconut and encourage Xander to take his usual jelly.

I feel pretty good as we all eat the donuts around the conference table. Kelly gets a little powdered sugar on her cheek and I covertly motion for her to dust it off. She does so with an appreciative smile.

I keep glancing over at Xander eating his jelly donut. At one point, he catches me looking at him.

"Good donut?"

"Mmm," he says with his mouth full. He's nearly done.

"Should be," I say, then pause for effect. "I just violated it in the car."

The room is silent for a beat and I feel my heart pounding in my ears. Then everyone cracks up. I mean really cracks up. Like they can't believe me of all people would go there. It's a really big laugh.

The only person not laughing is Xander. His mouth is full of donut and his bright eyes look at me with confusion. He wants permission to laugh too but he's not gonna get it from me.

"What? Didn't you notice how misshapen it was?" I ask him innocently. "You think I'm kidding? In most states, that jelly donut and I are practically married now."

It's the coup de grâce. The room explodes. It's the biggest laugh we've ever had for sure. Everyone's too busy cracking up to pay Xander much mind as he stumbles to his feet coughing and clearing his throat, fluttering out of the room towards the bathroom. Phil is gasping for breath he's laughing so hard.

Kelly is squealing, rocking back and forth in her chair, face red and wet and for the first time in 20 years I want a cigarette. I wish Fitzy was around to hear this. I lean back, try to enjoy the

moment. This will be over before I know it.

BLACK CAR

WE MEET AT A MOTEL ROOM A STONE'S THROW from the highway in the valley. I could've afforded nicer but something about the seediness of the place seemed appropriate. Maybe even a little fun.

It wasn't without its charms and was leaning into the retro '50s thing with a boxy faux-vintage radio on the night stand and wallpaper that reminded me of *The Jetsons*. The over-chlorinated pool sparkled like a blue jewel out our window.

"Pool's nice," I say, collapsing on the bed after we'd gone at each other. Lauren liked to get right down to brass tacks. "I may even take a few laps before going back to work."

"Yeah right. If I get bed bugs, I'm going to kill you."

"I'll give you bed bugs." I make like I'm going to nibble her shoulder.

"Careful. You know you gave me a bit of a bruise last week."

She points to her shoulder. I make a sympathetic face but I don't see anything. My gut is she's being a drama queen.

"You bring it out in me."

"Ok, ok," she says.

27

I refill both our plastic cups with the CVS champagne I'd bought on the way here. Champagne was another seedy little tradition. We never even finished the bottle. It was just to have a glass as an ice breaker. I like getting to the room early. Fill up the ice bucket. Unwrap the plastic from the plastic cups. Strip off the comforter and shove it in the closet.

We joked about making a private Instagram account of all the funky little places we had met up. I joked, at least, and she smiled.

"It's like we're in a Graham Greene novel," I said once and she nodded.

I could have afforded better but again we weren't here for the amenities. I never booked at chains either even though I could use my points at a La Quinta.

"Want to squeeze in a tour of Hollywood star homes before heading back to work?" I say, holding up one of the shiny brochures fanned out on the bedside table. "Here's a coupon for a ribeye at The Smokehouse."

Plus, some trendy hotel downtown and who knows who we would run into. These weekly meet-ups add up as well and she's never offered to pitch in, not that I'd let her.

"The pool really does look nice. Maybe next time?"

"And get my hair wet in the middle of the day? You don't know much about women, do you?" She's putting on her bra. "I should be getting back."

"Already?"

"What? Did you want to watch HBO or something?"

Kind of, I think.

Then there's the convenience. My office is two miles away on surface streets and hers is three exits west. Neither of us is in a position to take multiple hour lunches.

Sometimes I look online for fun facts about the places we're staying. Like this one motel in Atwater was owned by Scientologists; supposedly The Doors once stayed in another. The Night Stalker was rumored to have spent a night in one but I didn't tell her that.

"Guess which Paul Thomas Anderson movie they shot here? The exteriors at least."

28

"Who's Paul Thomas Anderson?"

There's a slit where the turquoise drapes fail to meet and the midday sun bisects her face. Annoyed, she gets on her knees to pull them flush.

"Who's Paul Thomas Anderson? Who's Paul Thomas Anderson?"

I'm not really that worked up. The nice thing about this being just an affair is that Lauren not knowing who Paul Thomas Anderson is isn't my problem. Same with her not really laughing when I do a bit.

"Do you know who The Night Stalker was?"

Suddenly she jumps back and falls onto the bed. At first, I think she accidentally flashed someone passing by to the ice machine. Or saw a mouse, which would definitely be a strike against this place.

"What's wrong?"

"His car!"

"What?"

I hope I misheard her but her expression assures me I didn't.

"His. Car."

"Where?" I sit up.

"Don't look."

I pull on my boxer shorts. Scrunched up against the head board, she watches as I roll off the bed and crouch walk under the window. I exaggerate my stealth, humming the Mission Impossible theme. I want to keep things light. I wait till I'm at the curtain's edge to stand up flush to the lumpy retro wallpaper. From here my wedge of visibility includes the cement walkway outside the window, the empty courtyard pool a floor below us, a corner of the front office and enough of the parking lot to see a half dozen parked cars, gleaming like cartoon teeth in the sun and harmless enough.

"Scanning the perimeter."

I don't see his car.

My chest untightens a bit.

"Black Dodge thing, right? All tricked out," I say messing with her.

"Yeah." She sounds scared.

"That's not it." I laugh. "You really got my heart pumping. I think you were looking at that black Mustang."

"No. Not the Mustang. Look across the street."

I look again. Beyond the parking lot is a thin median and, how did I miss it, a tricked-out black Dodge, parked right underneath the neon motel sign, dormant in the daylight. The car's windows are tinted absurdly black. It's impossible to tell if it's parked or idling.

"Right." I try to appear calm. "Still it's hard to see from here. It might not be him."

"It's him."

"He's not the only black Dodge with tinted windows in the city."

"And black vintage plates."

"Really?" I peek again. "Even with that."

"I'd know that embarrassing midlife crises from a mile away," she says. "But say you're right and it's not him. You really want to put your pants on and walk out that door to find out?"

She makes a good point.

"Let's just take a beat and—" My phone buzzes and I start. I pick my pants up off the floor to fish it out and silence it when I see the Caller ID.

"Shit. It's him."

"What? Don't answer!"

It's buzzing in my hand like it's alive.

"Of course not. Or should I?"

And then it stops. I instantly think I should've answered it. Craig is something of an acquaintance. He could be calling me to play poker or something.

"Maybe he'll text."

"I should've answered it. Now we don't know why he was—"

The phone comes alive in my hand again. I hold up a finger for her to be silent and take a deep breath. Suddenly I can't remember how I usually answer the phone.

"Craig!" Definitely not like this. I sound completely phony.

It's quiet for beat. He coughs wetly.

"Lauren is fucking somebody."

"What?" I say sounding even more phony.

"I've been suspicious for weeks and I overheard her on the phone the other night." His voice cracks. I hear him pound what I assume is the dashboard. "Doesn't matter. Look I'm parked across from the Sea Breeze motel on Flower Street. I'm looking right at the room. No doubt she's with him right now."

Lauren is on her knees on the bed, mouthing at me to tell her what the hell he's saying. I need to concentrate and wave her away and turn my back.

"Maybe she's just—I mean are you sure? That doesn't sound like Lauren."

"Did you hear a word I said? I'm at the motel. Hell, I saw her go in there twenty minutes ago. The guy must've been in there already. Sea Breeze. You work pretty close to here right?"

I chew my lip. Is this a trap?

"Yeah. No. Yeah my office isn't too far."

"Look man, I have my Glock and some pretty bad thoughts in my head right now."

His Glock? He drops this like we talk guns all time.

"Hey could you come meet me?"

"Meet you?"

"I know it's a lot but I could use a buddy right now to talk me down."

Why is he asking me?

"Sure, I could—why don't I meet you for a drink. You know the FireFox Room a few blocks away?"

"No, no. I gotta watch the door. Look just meet me here. You'll see me. You know my car, right? Dodge. Tinted windows. Vintage plates."

"Who could forget."

"You'll come right? Quick. I don't want to do anything bad."

"Yeah, ok. Bad is not good. I'm on my way right now."

He hangs up.

"On your way?" she echoes.

I'm getting dressed not knowing what my next move is. Nothing like this has ever happened. So much for keeping it light.

"He doesn't know who you're in here with. He wants me to come comfort him or something!?"

"What!?"

"I know. I didn't know we were that close."

"He thinks you're clever or something. Fun bachelor guy."

"Maybe it's cause my office is close?" I wonder aloud.

"He doesn't have many friends."

"Ok. He's got his *Glock.*"

"Oh my god, oh my god."

"Don't get upset."

"I knew this was a fucking mistake. I've never done anything like this."

I don't point out the week before and the week before. I know what she means although I don't believe her.

This isn't my first rodeo either. I've been told I give off a certain vibe.

"Let's not play the blame game here." If we were going to play the blame game, I'd point out that technically she's the one having an affair. That's a last resort nuclear option.

"Blame game? Trust me, I know this is my fault. You're a fucking child. Do you even own a plant, Kyle?"

I think this is the first time she's used my name.

"I don't know what that has to do with anything." I'm running around the room trying to be proactive. "If there was just some other way out of here."

If this were a real hotel, I imagine ordering room service and smuggling myself out hidden under the bellhop's cart.

Maybe I should've sprung for better.

"Should I call the police?" she asks.

I guess it's preferable to being shot in the face but just slightly. We all live in the same rent-controlled building for chrissake. He laughs at my jokes in the elevator. If he didn't kill me, I'd still have to move.

"Hold it." I walk over to the back window where the A/C unit rattles, drooling coolant down the wallpaper. We're only on the second floor and below is a weed-strewn patch hidden from view.

"I could jump?"

"Are you crazy?"

"What choice do I have?"

"What about me?"

The second floor isn't so high, right? I think. I push hard as I can to crank open the window but before I can grab it, the sputtering air conditioner tilts backwards and falls. It crashes to the ground below with a thud but still it's all in one piece. Now I just need to avoid landing on it.

"I can't believe this," she says as I use the desk chair to climb out feet first. Then I awkwardly slide my body against the metal sill as I shimmy out and then hang from the ledge so I don't have far to fall. How many feet is half a story? It's windy out. My chest is hot against the prickly stucco and I hang there for a minute. Maybe I should've tied some sheets together like in a movie. I look up at Lauren's worried face. It's too late to back out now and my fingers are losing their grip.

I release them and use my hands to push off from the building a bit so I don't scrape myself on the wall going down. Except I do. I try to bend my knees but still land with one foot bent downward. Like a ballerina toppling over mid-pirouette. I hear a crack and I crumble to the dirt.

"Jesus? Are you ok?"

I steady myself on the dented air conditioner and straighten up. The clunky motel key jingles in my pocket. From this angle, the building's all chipped paint and water stains, like I'm looking at the backside of a neglected doll house.

Above me, Lauren protrudes from the window in only her bra. Her face is full of regret, about this and everything that came before.

"Never better."

"Well, what about me?"

"I'll get him away from here. You go back to work. Get a coworker to be your alibi. If he brings it up tonight, pretend you don't know what he's talking about. Says it's all in his mind. No one wants to believe the worst about their spouse!"

I wonder how many people in the motel are overhearing this flimsy plan.

I wave her back inside the window and she shakes her head and complies. That's probably the last I'll see of her for a while. I glance around to make sure no one saw me. Luckily the lot is mostly empty except for old soda cans and junk food wrappers

and a few yards away there's a mini homeless encampment with tattered tents trembling in the mid-day Santa Anas. You'd think the motel would do something about that.

My slacks and blue button-down are flecked with dirt but at least I'm not bleeding. My left foot is killing me and already swelling so fast my dress shoe is now unbearably tight. I pass a window with a naked man laying across his comforter. He's stroking it to cable news, too cheap to order a movie. Empty liquor bottles form a disjointed skyline across the room's furnishings like he's been there a while. He doesn't notice me.

I smooth my hair back and turn the corner around the motel.

There's the black car, shimmering in the traffic's fumes like a mirage. It's definitely a midlife crisis purchase. The sun is punishing as I dodge cars, limping across the street and come up on it from behind. Bass rattles the tinted windows.

I rap on the passenger side door. It unlocks.

"Came as fast as I could."

I drop into the passenger seat and am in another dimension. Industrial metal music is playing. The air-conditioning is blasting and it feels good to sit. The air is heavy with marijuana.

Craig is red-faced behind the wheel with a bottle of Early Times whiskey between his legs. Staring straight ahead, his sunglasses are on and his pock-marked cheeks are wet and greasy. He seems bigger, beefier than I remember sitting across from me now. Lauren says he never shuts up about CrossFit. His short sleeve shirt is clearly worn to show off his biceps. No matter how much he works out he still can't really pull off the look, like his muscles are a Halloween costume he's donned to distract from his blotchy skin and questionable personality. Same with the tinted windows and the cool guy car.

"Thanks for coming, amigo."

The gun sits barrel down in the cup holder. So that's what a Glock looks like.

"No worries. Sorry about the circumstances."

We sit there as he bobs his head to the music, one hand white-knuckling the wheel. He's showing me he's in pain and is man enough to not care that I know it. I'm reminded of what a

cheeseball Craig is.

That was my first impression when I met him and Lauren at the dog park adjacent to our building. That she was too hot for such a cheeseball. Even if their unit was on the top floor. Mine's on the ground level.

I remember him gripping my hand a little too tightly and laughing too hard at my lame jokes. But I accepted his offer to play poker with him and his realtor buddies a couple times. It was nice to have someone to laugh at my jokes. They were all married and wanted to know if I got a lot of pussy. They actually used that word.

"Let's just say we met in the dog park and this guy doesn't even have a dog!" Craig had elbowed me and everyone laughed

It got old quick.

A few days later Lauren came down to my unit to return the windbreaker I left behind. My lucky blue jacket; I wish I had it now.

"Fucking bitch," Craig says finally.

"Whoa, whoa."

A pine tree air freshener hangs from the mirror; the plastic wrapper is still half way on to modulate the freshness. Lauren hates that Craig does that. She says he's anal. He won't let the dog sleep in their bed even.

"I wanna kill her."

"That's just crazy talk. Will you listen to yourself? That's your wife you're talking about. You guys have been married how many years? You've got a great chocolate lab together."

"Kill her and whoever she's there with," he continues.

"Let's just chill. Put on some different music for starters."

"Fucking whore." He punches the roof of the car. "She made me a cuck."

"Are you sure she's even in there with someone? Maybe she just wanted to get some private time or use the pool?"

"That makes no sense. I mean, seriously, look at this dump!"

I make a show of tilting my head to check out the place.

"Not bad. Kinda cool and retro—"

"What?"

"Looks familiar. Like I recognize it from a Paul Thomas

Anderson movie or something?"

"It's a fucking dump, man!"

"Ok, ok."

"I just saw some guy in flip-flops smoking crack."

"Really? Huh."

I change tack.

"Listen, you've caught her red-handed but there's no reason to play this out in public, when everyone's tensions are high. That's when bad decisions get made."

He grunts.

My foot is killing me. I think I broke something.

"Come on. Nothing good is going to come from just sitting here. Let's go grab a drink, talk this out."

"I dunno."

"I know this one place close by with a good happy hour. The bartender makes the best old-fashioned. You'll love the waitresses there."

"Eh."

"Trust me on this."

He tosses his sunglasses on the dashboard and turns to me with red-rimmed eyes. He's staring right at me. I suddenly remember I lost those few times we played poker when Craig called my bluffs.

"You're probably right."

"That's the spirit." I exhale.

Everything will be better when we're away from this place, old-fashioned in hand. I'll text Lauren on the sly. Call the office and make up an excuse. Maybe rethink my romantic life a bit.

"You're a good guy Kyle." He's finally turned down the music.

"There's a first time for everything."

Actually, most people do think I'm a good guy. I keep things light. Lauren's wrong; I do have plants but not much else and this whole scenario is a good reminder why.

Craig casts a look up at the motel room. I can tell he's softening to my plan. I find myself looking forward to cheering Craig up, like I'm doing a good deed. There are worse things than being a jacked-up cheeseball with no irony.

"Ok, ok. I'll fix her goddamn ass later," he says. "Thanks Kyle. Seriously."

I feel guilty but I'm also curious. I mean a few poker games, some small talk in the elevator and dog park. I guess that constitutes a friendship nowadays. I want to ask if he would still have called me if my office wasn't in nearby Burbank? Like would he have called one his realtor buddies from poker night? A family friend? I want to ask but I'm not sure how.

"Next stop cocktails. Let's do this."

"Seriously though, Kyle. You're solid man. You're a good friend." He's definitely a bit drunk. Still though I can tell he's fishing for some kind of reciprocity.

I guess if I had a wife and she was screwing somebody and I was upset and going to call someone to talk about it, I can't say I have a very deep Rolodex.

"You're a good friend too, man." I'm gilding the lily a bit in the hopes that he'll hurry up and put the car in drive.

This is more affection than Lauren or I have ever expressed to each other in these last couple months. She's a pretty cold fish. Not only has she never offered to pay for the room, she barely even wants to talk. The waitresses really are pretty friendly at this bar and there's a chance I can even get Craig laid. That would make us both feel better. He's not a bad egg. Even if he is a little anal. Lauren's no picnic.

"You too, man. You too," he says as if I was the one who brought this whole thing up.

To drive his point home about how close we are he gives me a manly pat on the leg.

His meaty hand lands there with a clap above my knee. I don't even mind. Maybe it's the contact high of the weed but I feel a bit of bro affection for the guy. I don't have many friends either. But then his hand lingers.

For a split-second, I think Craig's feeling me up. Then I realize it's worse. He feels something.

It's the single key in my pocket attached to the kind of over-sized triangular keychains that only come with motel rooms.

A nicer hotel would never hand out something so clunky.

"Let's just chill buddy," I start.

37

Before I can move, Craig's hand bears down with all his massive weight and the outline of the key punctures my skin. His other hand is already on the gun.

BETTER THAN DRUGS

I STOP AT A GAS STATION MARKET OFF THE highway for Travis's favorite chewing gum, double-shot cappuccino and energy breakfast bars then gun my car across Delray Beach before the foam flattens.

The gate guard at Tranquility Bluffs has zero muscle tone and a man-bun. Past the gate it's a pretty plush set-up; all manicured hillsides, wooden walkways and charming bungalows. I spot some decent talent milling about, gnawing their nails like they just quit smoking and meditating in little matching pajama pants in a semi-circle by a dinky waterfall. I wonder how many are secretly high.

With his duffel bag slung over his shoulder, Travis is leaned coolly against a faux Greek column of the mothership building, putting out big man on campus vibes to no one in particular.

He almost looks healthy; trimmer for sure, bright-eyed, not screaming obscenities and tossing lit matches at me. It's humid as hell but, like always, he looks cool.

"What's up big boy? Going my way?!" I call out all sexy-like through my cracked tinted window. It's not the best joke but I'm

trying to keep things upbeat.

We're old friends but Travis is a pretty popular guy. I admit I was pretty pumped he texted me to come get him as opposed to Glenn or Rocket. He gets in my Nissan and slaps on his polarized shades.

"So, you meet anyone special in rehab?" Not loving how that sounds I instantly rephrase the question. "You know, crush some ass? Sink the pink?"

"It's not rehab. It's *reset*," Travis corrects me. "And fuck yeah I did."

I crank up a driving-home-from-rehab playlist I made just for this occasion, heavy on Travis's favorite artists. Of course, I don't tell him that. We speed down Federal Highway with the bass shuddering the windows like old times. Travis is antsy and keeps flexing his biceps like he wants me to compliment him.

"Must've had a good gym," I say, trying to be supportive.

"Twenty-three days clean and I'm on something better than drugs! I feel like the world's my fat yummy oyster. I'm ready to kick ass, take names, have kids, run for President. Who knows?!"

He does seem pretty bright-eyed and not drooling everywhere. Plus, he got mad laid and is looking in solid shape. Maybe it's my time to turn over a new lease on life. Or is it "leaf"? I stroke my chin. Either way it couldn't hurt to cut back a little here and there.

"The kicker is," Travis knocks on my dashboard, "insurance paid for it so, cha-ching!"

He explains the whole thing was a requirement of his severance package after getting too wasted at this year's office holiday party. Actually, there was no holiday party this year which made his behavior really stick out. Then there was the huffing ammonia in the wellness room with the hot intern incident.

"The direct mail marketing business used to have a sense of humor," he says through a mouthful of energy bar. "There whey in this?"

He spits it out the window before I can tell him I don't know. He's off caffeine now too so I drink both gigantic cappuccinos and eat all the chalky energy bars so I'm wired and nauseated

by the time we pull up to the curb in front of his favorite 50's-themed diner, Big Peachy's. At least, Big Peachy's *used* to be his favorite diner. Now he says he wants to avoid anything that could spark old habits, so apparently Big Peachy's and their "famous" Hangover Helper Belly Bomb Protein Platter is out. Through the Airstream's window, I see Big Peachy's welcoming smile turn to confusion and then hurt as we cruise right past and jaywalk across the street to a new 80's-themed diner with mirrored ceilings and waiters dressed like Miami Vice extras.

Travis orders blackened veal marsala, a side of fruit roll-ups and an energy soda for babies which he says is the strongest thing he drinks now. I just carb-load on their bottomless basket of Mr. T's sticky buns. What I really want is one of their "famous" Bloody Mary's which, according to the menu photo, comes with a jumbo shrimp, old-timey pickle, Rubik's cube and a certificate of purchase.

"Hot damn. Those bloody Mary's are something else." Travis watches one passing by us on a tray like a parade float before his blue eyes snap back to me. It feels like he's testing me. Travis is a tester and big into loyalty.

"Totally," I agree but hedge my bets. "Although seems a little unsanitary to me."

Travis laughs hard like I'm the last person in the world who should be judging what's sanitary and what's not, and he has a point. I'm a little bit of a slob but I put on a fresh shirt when it counts: like to go clubbing or upscale strip bars or for this occasion.

Even though I'm not hungry I keep shoveling in the sticky buns to keep from talking. This is probably the most time we've spent together sober since being pinned upside down in a car crash a few years ago. Everything I think of to say has to do with me being at a bar or snorting crushed stimulants off body parts at social events or coming out of black outs to find myself in a stranger's sunroom or visiting my great aunt in Orlando. Don't get me wrong—that's not how I spend the bulk of my time—but am I really supposed to prattle on about data entry or what shows I'm streaming? I pick at the menu's lamination.

"Started watching *Bones* again."

Travis nods. I hope he's not regretting having me pick him up at reset instead Glenn or Rocket.

"There's so much I missed the first time around and the leads have great chemistry. You can't fake chemistry."

Travis is packing away a sheet of sweaty lemon-drenched veal like nobody's business and texting his new friend Uncle Billy.

"Uncle Billy's not my real uncle," he explains. "He's like my reset uncle, like a guru or a big brother. He's been there, done that. He's gone to hell and back and doesn't suffer fools. I don't take a leak without asking Uncle Billy how many times to shake it."

"Sounds very cool. Can't wait to meet him."

"Honestly he wouldn't be a big fan of yours. I don't mean you, personally. I just mean your lifestyle, your brand, your general essence," he says. Sensing I'm hurt, he adds, "I appreciate you picking me up today, Rob."

"No worries. What are old friends for?"

I almost say 'drinking buddies' but catch myself. *Percocet Pals, Coke Compadres, Fentanyl Friends?*

"The thing is, being with you is a bit of spark for me, Rob." He explains that's a term he learned in reset.

"I mean if Uncle Billy could see me now." He shudders at the thought.

I shrug, a little sheepish. My mom always said Travis was a bad boy but not in a sexy way, which I always found odd that she felt the need to clarify; as well as a terrible influence who was screwing up my not-particularly-bright-anyway future, and I'd probably jump off a skyscraper if he did it first. "Not necessarily!" I'd scream back in hot tears.

I can't help being flattered that Travis feels I'm enough of an influence to spark him to do anything. This is even better than him texting me over the other guys to pick him up. I wonder if Rocket knows.

"What I'm saying is, it would be easier for me if I could just call you something else," he continues. "Like Brendan or Elijah."

"Okay," I say slowly, hoping those are just first draft examples and he's about to start spitballing some way cooler names. Like

Bradshaw or Lee.

"And maybe you could wear something different." He's eyeing my Marlins baseball cap and my ironed "Is it Friday yet?" t-shirt that I wore special for today. "Like, oh I don't know, a beret or Kente cloth."

"Not sure that fits my, like, aesthetic," I tell him. I have a lot of t-shirts alluding to what day of the week it is. "Plus, good luck finding any of that stuff around here."

"Actually, we passed a beret store a few strip malls back, Elijah."

It's a good thing Travis is such a close old friend cause even the coolest looking beret in the store makes me look like a d-bag, plus I do not look like an Elijah.

"Eli," he splits the difference when I push back. "Cause we're good friends."

He's right about that. I wouldn't mess with my signature look, eat lunch sober, and yank out my futon for just anyone.

Maybe this is the first little baby step of my new leaf, or lease, or whatever. Travis cleaning up his act might be a wake-up call for me to straighten up a skosh. Like when I invested heavily in cryptocurrency, took up Brazilian jiu-jitsu, waxed my chest or leased a cherry red Nissan Z because Travis did it first.

Back at my condo I stash some rainy day pills in a plastic bag lodged in my rectum, hammer a couple nails to seal tight the liquor cabinet and medicine drawers and tell Travis to kick back and make himself at mi casa.

"So. Want a breast milk smoothie?" I ask. "I get the milk through this chick on Facebook. Same shit they give premies. Fifty cents an ounce."

"That's a killer deal." Travis nods. "But no."

Turns out Travis has a lot of so-called sparks—breast milk, boogie boards, BBQ's, Fort Lauderdale, dance clubs, jiu-jitsu, airboats, pain clinics, CVS, jam bands, dog parks, protein powders, Bally's, actually all gym franchises, Shriners, *Bones*, Hawaiian shirts—so there's not a hell of a lot for us to do at my condo this weekend besides crank the air-conditioning, work out with kettle bells, eat egg whites and watch car chase clips

on YouTube.

Every few hours I snap my fingers like I just remembered something totally pressing I was supposed to do, and I slip off into the shoe closet or crawl under the futon to nibble a Xanny or sip recalled wine coolers.

"Just looking for my contact lens!" I'll burp from wherever I'm hiding.

Travis talks to Uncle Billy then sits on my back steps lighting matches. He borrows my Nissan Z to go to a hang-hang, which is what he calls his reset meetings, and then comes back and slams the door so hard, I bang a tooth on a wine cooler.

"I just want to bite everyone's freaking noses off!" he screams and kicks a small hole in my hall's wall. "I can't take another stinking second of this fresh hell!"

I'm hoping these are some of his reset Shibboleths which is what he calls their catchphrases. Or vice versa.

We're eating mushroom omelets, watching a stolen golf cart tear through its second spike strip on my favorite car chase channel when Travis tells he me has some rectifications to make. I put down the hot sauce and make an "I'm all ears" face.

"Before my reset I was occasionally violent and verbally abusive and that's something I want to acknowledge with you here," he says.

I nod like, good as gravy. The time he went ballistic on a bartender for serving him a whiskey sour in a curved little girly glass was literally the most scared I've ever been in a P.F. Changs.

But that, as they say, was a different time.

"I appreciate your acknowledgements," I say like I'm on some super serious reality show. I want to be a good friend here.

"I also want to assure you that I own past transgressions like, but in no way limited to, using your Q-tips, undercutting you with mutual friends by rolling my eyes when your name comes up, telling girls we both like that you have a dirty dick, acting like it's your turn to pick up the bar tab when it's mine, telling you my fraternity was prejudiced against guys with freckles when I was just trying to save us both some embarrassment, stealing your coke, hoarding the coke, basically a lot of coke-

related shady behavior, that bachelor party weekend when you screwed up getting the strippers and I made you give Glenn a lap dance, sucker-punching you that time we were pinned upside down in that car, pretending I didn't borrow your silky blue shirt when I totally did, giving your ex oral, pawning your stereo speakers, pissing on your bed that one time and telling you it was a piss burglar."

I'm unsure if he's done or taking a breath. I guess it could be worse, but it does raise a few questions.

"Which ex-girlfriend?"

"Wren or something like that."

"Wren is my current girlfriend."

"I see." He nods thoughtfully, eyes narrowed. "So, you've got her contact info then? That's good. I should make rectifications to her as well."

"It's ok. I can pass them on."

"I have to do them in person is the thing." Maybe he can sense my skepticism because he adds, "Uncle Billy says you have to follow the rules before you can break the faces of people who aren't following the rules."

I sigh like, of course. I can't really argue with that.

Travis is nursing a purple baby energy drink and FaceTiming Uncle Billy from the futon when Wren comes over after her night shift at the pharmacy with white wine and stolen prescriptions.

"Here's the thing, babe." I pull her into the kitchenette and explain the whole Travis situation. "Let's wait till Travis goes nighty-night on the futon before we break out the party favors."

"Maybe we slip something into his Babyade?" she asks. I hear the clink of plastic bottles as she rifles through her purse. "You know, get this party started."

I tell her to save that as a last resort. She makes a crying face and rubs her eyes with a clenched fist. Then we both split a bottle of vanilla extract to bide our time.

Wren and I met "cute" a couple years ago when I drove my Nissan Z over her mother's novelty birdhouse mailbox in Jupiter. I'm still unsure if it was a birdhouse shaped like a mailbox or

a mailbox done up like a birdhouse. I was pretty toasted and the thing was totaled, but it wasn't a complete loss. Somewhere between her calling the cops and me burrowing under her porch, we struck up a rapport and became an item.

"I heard Travis gave you oral." I was going to save this conversation for another time but the vanilla extract is doing a number on me.

"I heard you have a dirty dick."

"Touché."

I give her a little kiss to let her know it's all good in the hood. Part of our secret sauce is the way we accept each other warts and all; plus our love of getting totally hammered. And hey—better oral from Travis than, say, Glenn or Rocket. In fact, I'd be lying if I said I wasn't maybe a little flattered; Travis, as my mom always said, is kind of a stud muffin with magnetic eyes.

"That boy could sell ice to the Eskimos. Almost reminds me of your father," she'd say with a faraway look.

"What was he like?"

Then the faraway look would be replaced with a what-the-fuck-did-you-just-say look and she'd snap a wet dish towel in my face and tell me once and for all to stay the hell away from that no-good Travis!

"Adios Uncle Billy, you old wise piece of shit." Wren and I can hear Travis signing off from the futon area.

"Keep hitting your hang-hangs. Don't forget your Shibboleths," I hear Uncle Bill say back on speaker with a voice like sandpaper gargling gravel. "Text me in 5."

I explain to Wren that Travis made rectifications to me for, among other things, giving her oral and stealing my silky shirt and now he's probably going to make rectifications to her.

"Sweet," she says. "You don't mind?"

She seems giddy and I realize Wren may not be as familiar with all the rehab—or reset—terminology as I now am.

She and Travis go sit on the back stoop and light matches as I decide what kind of eggs to whip up for a late night snack. I land on scrambled but add some chopped veggies and spices to liven it up.

I'm suddenly feeling the need to step up my game with Wren. Who knows, when Travis moves off my futon, I may even suggest we take things to the next level. Travis cleaning up has inspired me, which could maybe inspire Wren. It could be like some beautiful holistic human centipede scenario with all of us sobering up, flying right and turning over new leeches. Maybe I could even convert that little nook off the den I use for coke and sketch sex into a baby bedroom.

I'm humming a nursery rhyme and setting the table when I hear the clatter of bent nails falling on peeling linoleum followed by the sharp snap of ice trays. I find Travis and Wren making frozen mudslides. As if breaking his sobriety isn't bad enough, there's one thing everyone knows and it's that frozen mudslides are Travis's danger zone. Vodka makes him breakdance and the heavy cream means he'll destroy my bathroom.

"Dude." I get between Travis and the plastic handle of Mexican vodka. "Don't make me call Uncle Billy!"

"It's after midnight." Travis laughs and gives me a duh look. "Mudslide Monday?"

As Wren fills the blender with clotted cream and Kahlua, she sings "California Dreamin" but substitutes the lyrics to Mudslide Monday.

"I know what day it is. But it's Me No Drinkie Monday for you, old pal." Alliteration is not my strong suit. "Wren and I want to be supportive. We can have a great time not drinking or doing anything fun and instead watching YouTube. I made spicy eggs."

"Kill me," Wren says.

Travis explains the restart school of thought behind sobriety which includes getting totally cross-eyed blotto one Monday a month. So blotto and faded that you're not tempted to drug, drink or even want to smell alcohol for at least another month.

"So a cheat day?"

"No, no, no," Travis corrects me. "This is based on hard science and a very special episode of *Diff'rent Strokes*."

I vaguely remember that one. Bet that show holds up like shit.

"Okay. I'm not gonna lie. This all seems a little screwy."

"You want to tell that to Uncle Billy?"

"Listen I'm not the mudslide police. I don't have a PhD in, you know, not getting fucked up on high-alcohol dessert drinks." Wren snorts as if to say 'I'll say' which then she does say as well.

"I just—

I'm cut off by the growl of the blender and soon a frosty mug of creamy chunky alcoholic goodness is numbing my hand. I swill the frothy nectar until I have an ice cream headache, then pour another. Wren breaks out some blotter acid and generic Adderall and I start screaming so I can sound good and hoarse when I call into work sick in a few hours. Travis is like a drill sergeant assuring us the harder we party now, the less painful his next month will be. I do my best to be a good friend.

The sun's coming up or is it going down as I wake up on the futon. Or *in* the futon. It's like someone didn't see me passed out and tried with all their weight to fold me into the couch, almost snapping my arm off in the process.

The condo isn't looking so hot—my flat screen is dripping blood, a nitrous tank is lodged into the wall and someone drank all my high-end breast milk and used old family photos to chop lines. I wonder if Glenn or Rocket came over. My head feels like I'm being operated on and I'm fairly certain there's gunk in my pants. Like old times but not in a good way.

Travis is in my bed. As is Wren. They're both passed out head to toe but not like you do when you're being chaste at a middle-school sleepover and more like when you conk out mid-sex act with someone else's girlfriend. The room stinks of off-brand Irish cream and night sweats, maybe even some ass play. I crack a window but don't turn on a light.

I'm too hungover for details.

I chug a Bud Lite to get my bearings and run a lukewarm bath. I know this feeling well and there's nothing to do but listen to murder podcasts with frozen peas on my head until I feel ready to face whatever remains of the day. So much for new leafs and leases.

I'm not sure when but at some point, Travis sits down on the lip of the tub, right on my jerking off hand.

"Ow."

"Do you know the reason I called and asked you to pick me up at Tranquility Bluffs?"

"Because Glen doesn't have a car? Cause we're old friends? Maybe even best friends?"

"Because I knew how easy it would be to muck-wallow with you. Muck-wallow is what we call backsliding."

"Ok." My hand was going numb.

"You know your problem Elijah?" he asks. "You're the worst kind of an enabler. In reset you're what we call a Toxic Tommy. It's the biggest spark there is."

I sip my Bud Light, feeling a lecture coming on. Travis waltzes us down memory lane. Choking each other purple in high school, refilling our respective stepdads' bourbon bottles with iced tea and little dribbles of piss, showing our dicks to the school custodian in exchange for sticky hash-coated Swedish Fish. Later were keggers with opiates, bachelor parties on Windex and speedballs, baby showers and fishing trips powered by mescaline with Glenn and Rocket. In each example, Travis fingers me as the instigator.

"Hell, I just wanted to catch my first bass." Travis looks like he's actually wiping a tear off his cheek. I tear my hand from under him and do the same except the tears keep coming for me. I sink down deeper into the tub.

"Maybe it's time for you to pull yourself up by your shoe tassels," he says, then clarifies. "That's what we call turning over a new leaf to get a lease on life."

My hangover is still roiling like an electrical storm when Travis and Wren drive me to Tranquility Bluffs later that day in my Nissan Z. I play the same special playlist but in reverse. I'm scared but also terrified but also really hungover as well as even a little hopeful.

"You got this buddy," Travis says.

I look back at Travis standing there waving goodbye, still looking cool and trim and definitely conscious and not drooling, with Wren by his side.

I take a mental picture and feel like I have something to

aspire to.

I watch them driving away until they've disappeared and then I step up to the big white front desk to check in for my restart. The dopey kid behind the counter calls it rehab. I assume he's new and don't correct him.

QUÉBEC

I HADN'T BEEN OUT MY APARTMENT MUCH
that winter when I met her at a party. I'm not exactly a party
person and was busying myself finding a cracker or anything to
leverage some dip with when she said to stop staring at her.

"Ha, ha!" She had a witch's laugh. "I'm screwing with you.
Stare all you want."

"Me?" I had made myself go to the party but had forgotten
to prepare for talking to people.

She told me I probably recognized her from the commercial
where she played the girl on the bus with headphones on, eating a
submarine sandwich. She did a little dance and mimed eating
an impossibly huge sandwich.

"Can you imagine someone actually doing that? Who
writes that shit?"

By now I'd assumed she was talking to me because there
was no one else in the hall. Her chapped lips were circled with
holiday punch and her tumbleweed hair was held in place by one
strained strand tucked behind her little ear. She took my phone
and followed a handful of accounts on Instagram that she said I

would find repulsive but in a fun way. One was a septuagenarian porn star with a plastic surgery addiction, another a toothless collector of botched taxidermy plus an obese woman bottle-feeding her possum.

"Instagram must've taken down the photo where she's breastfeeding that giant rat," she said, disappointed and scrolling.

I never found that cracker but on the subway ride home from the party I unfollowed all those unfortunate people except for the girl; she had used my phone to follow herself which I thought was a clever and forward way to connect us and who was I not to reach out and ask if I could buy her a beer.

On our first date she had me sit on the couch with her and run lines for a big audition for another sandwich spot. "I'm getting typecast cause I can open my jaw wide," she said and stuck a socked foot in my face. "Don't get any ideas, perv boy."

She complimented my line readings and filled our mason jars with red wine and told me this would only take a couple hours. "And don't think I don't know what you're thinking right now! Another crazy fucking actress."

She never sat still and took pride in calling herself out on things before anyone else could.

"I know my laugh is over the top so stop looking at me like you want to kill me" or "Don't think I don't remember that I said I was only going to have one drink at dinner" or "Just because I have X amount of cats doesn't make me a cat lady."

We would sit down to eat a dinner she destroyed her kitchen in the process of making. Before I could even try it, she'd shove a bite in her mouth and proclaim it a disaster. "Don't eat that!" She'd hustle the plate out from under my fork with beet-stained hands, toss the entire dish in the garbage like it was rat poison and tell me to open another bottle of wine. I'd do as I was told, curious to see what would happen next.

The first time she came with me, she threw me off her, darted out of the bedroom and returned seconds later in a turtleneck and sweats, crunching through a bowl of cartoon cereal like she'd just been binging a TV show. "Oh what? So now I'm the selfish lover?!" she accused me through a mouthful

of purple cereal. "Oh god that word! *Lover!* Gross, gross, gross!"

She called me "perv boy" when I kissed her and "Judge Judgey" if I didn't say anything and "Mr. Scratchy Beard" when she introduced me to people.

She had a funky tattoo on her shoulder that looked like a cross between a turd and Mr. Potato Head. "It's a turd," she snapped when I asked, then shook her head at me. "Come on. Who's ever heard of a turd with eyeballs?"

One time in bed she told me my penis lolled to one side like her boyfriend's in Quebec. His is a little bigger though, she added. This time I may have looked at her a little like I wanted to kill her. "I'm kidding" she screamed and did her witch's laugh. "You should've seen your face! You should've seen your face!" Then she thrust her tumbleweed of hair into the crook of my arm and explained she made dumb jokes like that when she was afraid and liked someone. I kissed her purple-stained mouth. "Oh, perv boy."

She told me I had negative thinking patterns as well as anti-social tendencies and was always loaning me self-help books and demanding them back if I hadn't read them the next day. Out in public, she accused me of flirting with any woman that talked to me. "Who? That woman with the clipboard?" I'd ask. She blamed her jealousy on her OCD which didn't make much sense if you saw her bathroom. I'd tell her she was the only weirdo for me and she'd say I make the jokes around here.

She cranked Fox News up loud and yelled at me that she was learning how the enemy thought and that I needed to get out of my bubble. She was vegan unless it was after midnight on a weekend—then, she'd howl drunkenly for pepperoni pizza. "I know! I know! But how many cows did you save this week?" She had a crush on Bela Lugosi and was endlessly disappointed by my hair, no matter how she positioned it, didn't have a widow's peak.

Before I could decide if something bothered me, she'd already accused me of resenting her for it, thrown up her hands as if to say that was just who she was, then lasso her boney arms around me and lick my face like a dog and ask if I could still stomach the sight of her for even one second longer. I could.

We sometimes fought for hours, broke up and got back together without me uttering a word. I thought about the nature show I used to watch as a kid about birding, how patience and no sudden movements for hours could yield such beauty and flashes of joy.

"It's not a turd. It's one of the California Raisins. You know the raisins from the '80s who sang Motown songs," she said late one night sitting on the side of the bed in the dark. "My dad loved them."
"Like the cartoons?" I was half asleep. "Or Claymation?"
"The last thing he said to me was to sing the California Raisins song. They were like his favorite band." She had her back towards me and I reached up and rubbed it. "I don't even think he knew who I was at that point."

Eventually she stopped throwing me off her to go eat cereal after she came and I'd gratefully wrap up my side of things lickety-split. If I saw her staring at me jealously at a party or drug store, I'd let my jaw go slack and roll my eyes back until whatever female was talking to me hurried away in embarrassment. That made her laugh. I'd pick up a bag of tacos on my way to her apartment, hiding them in my coat pocket and pretending to find them like magic after she flung our dinner away. When she told me to stop looking at her like I wanted to kill her, I'd roll on top of her and smother her with a pillow. "Are you dead yet, baby?" I'd ask then lift the pillow up. Her face would be red, mostly with laughter. I'd do this over and over, tickling her and kissing her face before clamping the pillow over it again. "Dead yet, baby?" I became mostly vegan too and even watched Fox News ironically with her. What a holiday from myself it was to be the normal one for once.

She flew off one day for a commercial shoot in Los Angeles—this one for double-cheeseburgers. She said that was a step up from sub sandwiches. We exchanged pet memes over text daily and one night she left a message of her singing "American Girl" at a karaoke bar but she was substituting in the

words "Perv Boy." Later in the week I noticed on her Instagram that she was in Quebec. She was cooking dinner in a beautiful apartment with brick walls and hanging plants—her hands red with beet juice.

"You know... My boyfriend," she said when I asked her over the phone about who took the picture. I said I was confused and she explained in an exasperated tone that she told me all about her boyfriend.

"You said you were kidding?" I answered.

"I was kidding about him having a bigger penis. Who would say something like that? Like I would actually measure anyway. Why do think I'm always wearing a beret?" She did her witch laugh. "I know I need a new laugh. Did you read that Eckhart Tolle book I gave you yet? Otherwise, can you send it to me?"

I didn't make a big deal about it but we didn't really talk after that. I went back to not leaving my apartment and ran her joke over and over in my mind. I wondered if he had a widow's peak too. I found the old nature show about birders online and re-watched my favorite episodes repeatedly.

I wanted to read the Eckhart Tolle book but didn't want to give her the satisfaction so I dropped it with no envelope in a mailbox I slunk by one afternoon. The book landed with a surprisingly loud thud; apparently, there were no letters to soften its fall. Much later, winter again, I slowed down, realizing I was passing by that same mailbox. I stood there and shivered, wondering if the book was still in there, untouched at the bottom.

EXTERMINATOR

NATHAN OPENED THE DOOR AND WAS surprised the exterminator was a woman.

"You're Lubkin Brothers Pest Control?" He said it with a smile.

"That's right. Think anyone wants to make this the face of the company." She motioned to herself. Her cheeks were ruddy like a cartoon drunk and she wore a too small blue work shirt with the name "Pepper" stitched over the breast.

"Well, thanks for coming on short notice."

She bustled past him, her body odor filled the foyer and reminded him of the one time he smelled a freshly dug grave. On the back of her shirt was the company logo: WE DON'T REST UNTIL WE KILL YOUR PESTS.

"Great place. I love a colonial. Classic house like this in such a hot neighborhood. You must know what you're doing."

"We got lucky."

His wife had fallen in love with the house. "We've been looking for something classic but still rustic," she'd said to the realtor, spinning on her heel and taking in the high-ceiling'd

living room with dark beams and a view of the woods. Nathan had nodded along even though he had never used the word "rustic" in his life. It did seem like a nice place to come home to every night after working long hours in the city, an escape. That was before he had been let go.

"This house has great bones. Quite the castle fit for a king," the exterminator said. She was knocking on the walls, squinting at book spines, running a finger along Nathan's stereo components. She left her Styrofoam cup of coffee on the end table, and when he thought she wasn't looking, he slipped a New Yorker cartoon coaster under it.

"You home sick today or what?"

Nathan felt her gaze on his black warm-up pants and faded I'm With Her t-shirt. He should have at least put on shoes.

"No, no. I do a lot of freelance work from home. I'm a graphic design—"

"This your wife?"

She picked up a framed photo off the book shelf of he and Holly on a white sand beach.

Nathan didn't love the disbelief in her voice.

"That's from our honeymoon in the Maldives."

"Real smoke show." She whistled low. "She an actress or what?"

"Ha. No, she's a lawyer."

"Even better. Can she take care of a DUI for me?"

"She's not that kind of lawyer. Copyrights and stuff."

"Where's your crawl space?"

"Um—"

"Don't hurt yourself." She grabbed her coffee and headed back outside. "I'll find it."

Two nights prior Holly screamed from the shower when he was cooking mushroom piccata. She said she saw a tail, pink and shiny, protruding from under the cabinet. Armed with a golf putter and a can of insect repellent, Nathan braved the foggy bathroom as she shut the door behind him, sealing him in.

"I feel like I'm in *Gladiator* or something."

"Do you see it? Do you see it?" she kept asking.

"Not yet. I'm looking everywhere."

Nathan moved his feet to simulate walking around but he remained pressed against the wall by the door. He didn't like the idea of killing anything.

When they first started dated, Holly had laughed at the lengths he went to gathering up a spider atop a magazine to transport it outside his dorm room. Like many elements of their relationship, Nathan was fairly certain she no longer found that endearing.

"I don't see the little fucker. Must be long gone. Probably hitched a drain pipe to the coast."

"You're gonna take care of this right, Nathan?" she asked later in bed.

The expensive ceiling fan he still hadn't installed sat in its box by the dresser; an in plain sight reminder of the other dozen botched or aborted home projects on his to-do list. One of the many surprises of marriage for Nathan had been just how ill-equipped he was for home ownership. He had grown up in a high-rise in Yonkers with his mother and two older sisters and suddenly he was supposed to know all about circuit breakers, sump pumps, foundations and lawn fertilizers. Now groaning pipes and flickering bulbs put him on edge. He lived in fear of a drip from the ceiling or warping floor board to torpedo his week and expose further incompetence. Over the holidays Holly had drunkenly teased him in front of her family for hiring someone through an app to light the heater pilot light.

Now he kissed her hard. "I'm on it, babe."

Standing in front of a towering wall of pest-related products at Home Depot in Stamford the next day, he listened to a burly clerk run through a variety of options. He looked like the kind of too on the nose handyman who would come to the door in a porno. Nathan had almost never watched pornography before he started working from home.

"... then you got glue traps which are good at catching them but the downside is you have to deal with them wriggling around. I like these zap boxes but you need to be vigilant about cleaning them after every kill cause the urine will short circuit

the sensors—"

"Jesus," Nathan said. It had felt so primitive. "What's the least painful solution?

The clerk raised his eyebrows. "For the rat or you?"

The crawl space turned out to be on the west side of the house. The afternoons were just starting to get cold. He hovered there, rubbing his hands, as the exterminator unsheathed a flashlight, tied a filthy bandana over her face and sunk to her knees, half her body disappearing under their old house.

"Holy fuck!"

"What?"

"You don't even want to know."

She crawled further. Her work shirt rose up across her back, her shapeless brown pants pulled the opposite direction. *What the hell was that?* Her lower back was awash in tattoos, some blurry and borderline infected-looking, others professional and intricate. Most so large it was hard to get more than a partial glimpse. It was like trying to read a map both upside down and only partially unfurled. Nathan stepped closer and twisted his neck to get a better look.

"Shit," she kept saying. "This is so bad."

He could make out a set of fangs dripping blood and a skull oozing snakes. And was that a sword shaped like an inverted crucifix? Were those numerals in Russian? German?

She squirmed deeper. Nathan was surprised by the sudden appearance of a dainty red thong bisecting both the disturbing mural and her surprisingly taut and appealing butt cheeks. Forgetting himself, he leaned in more, intimately close.

"Getting a nice show?"

She rolled out and onto her kneels in a brisk single motion that left Nathan stumbling backwards. He assumed a quizzical expression but he could feel his inflamed face gave him away.

"No offense but soy boys with baby hands don't wet my whistle."

"Excuse me?"

"I'm just messing with you. Let's talk turkey."

She was on her feet now, waving a gloved finger with a

glistening black glob in his face.

"See that? It's rat scat. There's mountains of it down there. Lucky you called me when you did."

"That so?" Nathan knew he had the wide open face of an easy mark.

Every time he got in his Chevy Bolt, he remembered his father-in-law joking to bring lube to the dealership next time because he had been so taken advantage of. Nathan had been annoyed at Holly for telling her father how much his lease payments were anyway.

He told himself he wasn't going to just roll over this time. He widened his stance. "So what kind of system do you use?"

She exhaled and gave him a tired look like her process was too complex for a civilian.

"Like is there a way to live trap them?" Nathan pressed. He figured if he was going to be paying for the service, it should at least be humane.

"Oh sure. I use these customized eco-traps—"

"Great."

"—and then I transport them outside the city to this little rat spa with trails and a pool."

Her laugh sounded like a bird attacking. Her broad shoulders bobbed like pistons.

"Ever hear of rat bite fever? Typhus? The Bubonic Plague?"

"Of course."

"You don't want to take chances when you're trying to bake up a newborn."

"How did—"

"C'mon. Young virile couple like yourselves." She gave him an exaggerated wink.

Nathan was embarrassed, assuming he had left the fertility doctor's paperwork on the dining table.

She scribbled out an estimate on a yellowed business card, her penmanship spastic like a child's, then handed it to him.

"Oh no, no, no …"

"Nathan." She stepped close. "Winter's coming and your place is vermin Club Med."

Her wretched breath was hot and cut with sweet candy

schnapps. "You know what a rat king is?"

He shook his head, a little dizzy by her proximity.

"It's when the rodent density is so high a bunch of rats get their tails intertwined and knotted together, creating one huge mad roving monster."

"Uck. That's disgusting."

"Imagine your little hottie wife waking up in bed to that?"

She left him shivering on the front porch with the estimate and, Nathan was fairly certain, the remnants of a monster fart.

He could still hear her chuckling as she reversed her black van down the driveway.

That night Nathan made a lentil, chard and sweet potato curry with ingredients he picked up from the town's sleepy midweek farmers market. The farmers market, the cheese and wine shop, a VFW bar that was never open and a handful of antique shops that felt more like someone's hobby than a business; there wasn't much in their town.

"Ivan did the funniest impression of Richardson at work today," Holly said as she came in the front door and hung up her coat.

Nathan had noticed Holly's coworker at the firm was always doing funny impressions of fellow lawyers and hard-ass clients. This Ivan often recommended prestige TV shows and online workouts as well, sending funny dog videos to Holly at all hours. Both times he met Ivan at work functions in the city, Ivan had called him Matthew.

"Oh yeah!" he shouted from the kitchen, wanting to sound game.

"Although I guess you have to know Richardson to get it," Holly backtracked. She headed straight for the bathroom to freshen up. "Oh, did you get a chance to take care of our little unwanted visitor?"

"Oh yeah. I'm on it, babe." Leaned over the burners, Nathan concentrated on the curry. "Loaded up at the Depot. Set some traps. His days are numbered."

"Or hers."

"Right. Ha. Theirs."

"Something smells good!" He heard her close the bathroom

door.

Nathan was plating dinner when he looked up and saw Holly standing in the doorway staring him down, the white bathroom waste basket in her hand.

"What the hell is this?"

Nathan wiped his hands on his apron and peered inside the basket she held at an angle for his benefit.

Blood was everywhere. A mountain of red toilet paper highlighted the tampon in the middle.

The pan behind him started to hiss.

"That…" He nodded thoughtfully. "Must be the exterminator's."

Even wearing headphones blasting one of his instrumentals-only playlists at his standing desk, Nathan had trouble concentrating on work when the exterminator was there and she was always there that week, the tools in her utility belt jingling, her battered boom box blasting nightmare inducing black metal.

She would circle to the back of the house through the woods at all hours, letting herself in and out through the basement bulkhead doors. One morning he was on the toilet noticing a white strand in his pubic hair when he heard, from right above him, the attic's floorboards creak under her weight. More than once he was gazing out his office window at the dull skies and noticed her smoking a cigarette in the woods, watching him.

"Takes longer than I thought to set a few traps?" Nathan wondered aloud to her in the kitchen one morning, making himself a matcha tea. "Want some?"

Pepper wanted black coffee and explained she had to patch the holes, install door sweeps, caulk windows, run mesh through the crawl space and cap the chimney before she could set any traps.

"You can't rush the hunt."

He took some medium roast beans out of the freezer to grind. "Gotcha," he said, not wanting to push the issue; at least not just yet.

"We popped our cherry!"

Pepper descended from the attic early one evening shaking a big plastic bag heavy with, presumably, dead rats. Startled, Nathan looked up from cooking a new recipe from the Times. He hadn't even known she was there.

"I guess that's positive. How many are in there?"

"What's cooking, good-looking?"

She hovered in the kitchen doorway, bag slung over her shoulder like Santa.

"It's a teriyaki tempeh with couscous."

"Smells better than it sounds."

"Well." Nathan hesitated. "My wife's working late if you'd like some."

"Really? Thanks."

The exterminator smiled, which was rare for her, but Nathan didn't see it. He was busy bending down and selecting the right Tupperware container to put her dinner into.

Her smiled had faded by the time he filled the container with a generous portion and handed it to her.

"You know," she said. "Your wife works late a lot."

"Lawyers, right."

"You're very trusting."

"Excuse me?"

"Sometimes the rats aren't just living under your floor boards." She shrugged. "But that's just my life philosophy."

"Seriously? You can't just say something like that to a person."

Shaking his head, Nathan turned from the stove to face her, with her shit fingernails and bag of rats. He wanted to rip the Tupperware back from her. "You know what? I'm sorry but I think tomorrow should probably be your last day."

"Say what?" She shifted her weight. "I still got a lot of work to do."

"Then hurry up and get it done." Nathan was surprised by the edge in his voice. "It's not exactly rocket science is it."

Pepper's lids grew heavy over her eyes. The crinkle of the trash bag was audible as her fist tightened around it. Nathan tensed up under her gaze. He felt himself eyeing the pan on the stove top just to confirm it was in reach.

"Whatever you say." She walked out. "Thanks a million for

the vegetables."

Nathan awoke to a twisted silhouette filling his doorway. As the figure crossed into his bedroom, Nathan saw it dragged a thick tail behind it that extended far into the hall. Before the giant rat was upon him, he glanced over at Holly. Her eyes were bulging as she looked at him, pleadingly. Two other giant rats pinned her down. Nathan went to scream but an oily paw covered his mouth.

"Nathan."

Holly was shaking him.

It was too dark to see her expression. Nathan assumed she was waking him up from his nightmare but instead she motioned towards the walls.

"Do you hear that?"

There was scratching. Dozens of claws. Furious thrashing about and high-pitched noises. The chaos felt like it could splinter out of the walls and into their bed at any moment.

"Are those the rats? It sounds they're going mad in there," Holly said. "Jesus Nathan, you said you would take care of this."

"I will. I am."

"I'm putting in my ear plugs." She had her back to him now. "Some of us have to work tomorrow."

When Pepper arrived Monday to pick up her traps, Nathan confronted her in the kitchen. He was fully dressed, wearing shoes. He hadn't eaten breakfast to make him *hangry*.

"You said you wanted me to hurry up and 'get it done,'" she imitated his voice. "So I sealed up all the holes and trapped them in the walls."

"What? You know that's not what I meant."

"Calm down. They'll start eating each other to death in a day or two. Problem solved. *It's not exactly rocket science now, is it.*"

"Gross. That's not what I want. Look just do it the right way."

"If I'm gonna start all over, I'll need another check."

"You said you were going to take care of this. I'm not paying another dime. I'll call your boss. I'll write the world's

worst Yelp review. I'll tweet that you're the worst exterminator in Connecticut."

Nathan hated to pull rank like this. It took everything he had.

For once Pepper was silent. Then she burst out laughing.

"Holy shit. What a Karen," she said. "I'll get back to work and finish this up. But not because of that little hissy fit but because I know you're going through some stuff."

"I'm not going through anything."

"That's what you think. The world's worst Yelp review? You're hilarious."

"What's so funny about that?"

She laughed even harder.

"You kill me, Nathan. I gotta use your bathroom."

She took off her tool belt and laid it on the kitchen counter by her cup of coffee. He could still hear her laughing as she got situated on the bowl.

"Bitch," Nathan said quietly.

He opened a cabinet to make himself oatmeal when his eyes fell on the tool belt with its many little pockets, some of the flaps of which were open. He saw the Slim Jims she used to bait traps, the stun gun she liked to twirl on her finger cowboy style, a Bowie knife.

A bright orange packet of poison with a cartoon rat, huge XX's where his eyes should be, protruded from one pocket.

Before Nathan could think about it, he slipped the plastic lid off the cup and shook the little bag over the coffee. Three quick shakes dropped a tablespoon's worth of the chunky brown pellets into the dark liquid. The coffee bubbled as the pellets sank. Then there was the toilet flush and with shaking hands he hastily replaced both the coffee's lid and the plastic baggie into the proper pocket in her belt.

Pepper was still laughing and the sight of him, beaded with perspiration and loitering in his own kitchen, sent her into hysterics.

"Oh, please Nathan don't write a mean tweet. Whatever shall I do." She strapped on her belt. "Sweet Jesus. No wonder this country's going to hell."

Nathan wanted to see her swill the coffee and feel the pain or the burning or whatever the hell rat poison does as she looked at him with shocked eyes and sank to her knees, spewing blood on their blonde wood flooring.

She went to take a sip, her body still vibrating with giggles. Before the cup touched her lips, Nathan lunged forward and slapped it out of her hand. Hot coffee splattered across the kitchen; the empty Styrofoam cup spun like a top on the floor.

Pepper's eyes stretched wide as she took a big step towards Nathan. He flinched.

"I'm sorry." His voice quivered.

She wiped her wet hand on her pants and glared.

"Fucking pussy," he heard her say as she walked down the basement steps.

Nathan made butternut squash stuffed shells for dinner for the four of them. Holly had invited Ivan over. He brought a date, an attractive Argentinian photographer he met recently at his gym in Brooklyn, who didn't talk much and used the bathroom a lot.

"Nice to get out of the city for once. Country living," Ivan said looking around. "I could get used to this."

Distracted, Nathan had trouble keeping up with the conversation that night, riddled as it was with private jokes, copyright terms and legalese.

Ivan punctuated the conversation with asides to Nathan about what an animal his wife was.

"I mean seriously, Nathan." He pointed his knife at him. "Your wife is killing it at work. She is killing it. Total animal."

"Ivan."

"It's true. It's hard to keep up."

Nathan smiled in agreement.

"Usually I don't like vegan food but this is pretty good." Ivan took a huge bite to show his enthusiasm.

Then there was a scream. Lucia came running out of the bathroom.

"There's something in there!"

"Another rat," Holly said, then glanced, embarrassed, at

Ivan. "I mean mouse."

"Want me to handle it?" Ivan looked at her with bedroom eyes.

"Damn it. Nathan, this is ridiculous. You need to fire this exterminator. You know what? I'll call her right now. What's her number?"

"It's not a mouse. Or a rat!" Lucia corrected her. She stood at the corner of the table, too worked up to sit. Ivan rested a comforting hand on her shapely backside.

"It was a bunch of rats. All tied together somehow." She tried to demonstrate linking her fingers from one hand with another and pulling. She was trembling, her jewelry shook. "It's hissing and thrashing and horrible."

"A rat king." As if in a trance, Nathan stood up, his dinner fork still in his hand as he quietly walked off.

No one paid him much mind. Ivan helped Lucia back to her seat, rubbing her bare shoulders and Holly apologized profusely, said the upstairs bathroom was available and poured everyone more natural wine.

There was a crashing sound from the bathroom. A picture falling off the wall. Then a series of bumps like something was being slammed against the door.

Before anyone could say anything, Nathan returned.

It wasn't until he had tucked himself into his seat that they saw the speckles of blood on his face and glasses. There was blood on his pressed blue shirt's collar as well. But most upsetting was the fork he had taken into the bathroom. It was covered in blood and pulp and Nathan was quietly using it to eat his butternut squash shells with. For a moment it was silent except for the sound of him chewing. Then Lucia started to gag and Ivan comforted her. Nathan looked up and saw Holly staring at him.

"What?" He winked with his mouth full. "I told you, babe. I'm on it."

THE CULT IN MY GARAGE

MY HUSBAND WARNED ME HIS OLD COLLEGE
buddy who was coming to stay for a couple days was a real
handful.

"Boy, I could tell you some stories." He chuckled.

"Like what?"

"Well—" He looked at me and we both realized he couldn't
tell me these stories. I just refilled my coffee.

I'd had my fair share of my husband's old friends over the
years. They were all called things liked Sully, Gunner and Bobsled
with phlegmy laughs, wilting hair and beer guts threatening the
top button of their golf pants. They'd sit in the kitchen nook for
marathon tequila sessions reminiscing about smashing their car
into this tree or doing blow at that show, or after I'd gone to bed,
sticking their dick into so and so.

Middle-management blowhards or salesmen with one
passable suit, in town for conventions or seminars in nearby
Long Beach, who wanted to "see their bruh!" Each and every
one ruffled our young son Jonah's hair and asked him if he was
'getting any' in school. I couldn't help but notice the pale line

where they had twisted wedding bands off their fat fingers. One even wet the guest bed.

To my husband though they were fearless legends and master wits, stars of countless rip-roaring anecdotes that usually culminated in property damage and public defecation.

"She was a bit of a wallflower back in school," he'd say by way of apology for me and they would stifle a belch and nod politely like sure, sure and compliment the lovely wallpaper or the drapes as if throwing a dog a bone.

So, my expectations weren't exactly dashed when Owen from Phoenix showed up with a duffle bag and bottle of Cuervo, proceeded to get my name wrong and then bark for hours over the Weber grill about Jean-Claude Van Damme movies and college hockey with my husband.

Over dinner he scratched his graying stubble and was mercifully cryptic about his recent divorce and termination from his long-time sales job. He said he was ready for a big change in his life like he was saying something profound.

"Of course you are," my husband said. "Who isn't?"

"I mean I didn't major in philosophy just to spend my whole life selling off-brand soda to dollar store chains," he said in a moment of self-reflection that was rare at our dinner table.

"Course not. You majored in philosophy to get the punani!" My husband laughed with his mouthful of undercooked hamburger, shot me a quick conciliatory look and laughed some more.

For a split second I thought I saw Owen give me a little pity smile. A look that said he knew my pain and exhaustion but we all had our parts to play in this crazy life, crosses to bear, etc.

But then he started laughing too with his mouthful of hot dog and I realized the flickering kitchen bulb my husband still hadn't changed was playing tricks or maybe I'd had too much red wine and excused myself for bed and reminded them not to smoke weed inside or wake up Jonah with their war stories.

In the morning I noted to my husband that Owen had urinated a bit on the toilet seat and left beer rings on the coffee table.

"Give him a chance, babe. Owen's the real deal." He kissed my cheek. "He's kind of like the smartest guy I know."

I nodded and watched him leave for work with an egg stain on his tie. My husband's friends never failed to shine a spotlight on all his shortcomings to me.

I had dropped Jonah off at his special school and was writing copy for a new line of juicers in my office cranny when Owen said knock-knock and asked where he might find a screwdriver. At least he got my name right this time. As I was showing him the junk drawer, he thanked me for letting him stay in the garage which was news to me. I told him as much and went back to work. I was under deadline but kept getting distracted, watching him moving things in and out of our garage, listening to him banging and sawing away.

"It's just until he gets back on his feet." My husband had picked up my favorite Chinese dumplings for dinner as a peace offering. "He's had a tough couple years. He just needs to get his mojo back. He's like such a smart guy. He could have his own podcast or something."

"You said that already," I told him. "If he's so smart why can't he not dribble piss on the toilet seat."

I wasn't in the mood. My husband had lost a not insubstantial amount of our money a few years back investing it in another really smart friend's data-mining firm.

"He's not even going to use the house. He says he has everything he needs in the garage."

True to his word, Owen kept to himself. When I pulled shut our drapes at night, I would see a light still on through the garage door window. I would lie in bed wondering what he did all day and all night among all our recycling bins and neglected power tools.

"Hold it. Where does he go to the bathroom?" I asked one night but my husband was dead asleep.

I didn't see him again until I was returning from dropping

77

Jonah at his tutor's and he was coming out the side door with a pasty young woman in a faded sack dress. I straightened up.

One time some old friend of my husband's had brought a sex worker home after the bars closed and my husband and I heard them having sex on our new patio furniture. My husband insisted she wasn't a sex worker and this was while Jonah was just a baby, but still. I'm far from a prude but who wants something like that happening on your own furniture, even if it was outside.

And now I wasn't over the moon about it happening in my garage either.

So, I was preparing to not mince words when I noticed the way they were walking. He had his hand on her shoulder but in a brotherly way and she was holding a flyer.

"This is Penny," he declared when he saw me. "She lives in the brown unit at the end of the block with her mother who's been sick."

I didn't know what any of this had to do with me but said hello anyway.

"She came inside for a cold soda."

The mousey woman held up a can of blue soda to verify. A brand I'd never even heard of before.

"Okay then." What else do you say.

I went into the house to get to work but instead spied from the corner window as they said goodbye in the driveway. It was all very chaste, maybe for my benefit. But then Penny gave him a smile, it seemed so genuine, and turned to walk away, cupping the cheap soda like a votive candle.

"Hey a man's got to have friends, right?" my husband said when I told him. He seemed tickled. "Owen works fast. Just like back in school. A regular Mr. Popular."

"What about our son?" I said. "He has enough issues. I don't want Jonah being around whatever's going on in there."

"Jonah! Don't hang around the garage for now, okay!" my husband shouted in the direction of our son's room and then gave me a happy-now look.

The next day I saw more people. They came to the garage's

side door all stacked brows and pinched shoulders. One or two looked familiar. They rapped unsurely on the door, slipped inside and left an hour or two or three later with the same relieved smiles as that first girl, mouth blue and often cradling a soda.

That afternoon I was just about to give Jonah another warning to stay away from the garage when he uncrumpled a flyer he said he ripped off a telephone pole near his school.

"Isn't that our address?" he asked.

I nodded like it most certainly was.

I handed the same flyer to my husband that night as he was pulling a beer out of the fridge.

"*Alone? Depressed? Isolated? Well, me too!*" He read the flyer aloud and looked up. "Hey isn't this our address?"

I nodded like it most certainly was.

"Do we want lonely depressed people coming and going here all day?" I asked. "Don't we have enough already?"

"Well, at least he's not dealing drugs like you thought before. And he did specify 'the garage' in parentheses." My husband gave that last word an extraneous syllable. "He just needs a little more time to get back in the game. Let's cut him some slack."

"Some slack? When is he leaving?"

"I can't just kick him out on his butt."

"It's distracting. Do you know how much work I'm juggling?"

"But I got you those noise cancellation headphones on our anniversary."

"Is this really the hill you want to die on?" I'd read that phrase online and I always wanted to say it but my husband just looked confused.

"He's a good egg. I told you he practically saved my life that time on the jet skis, right?"

My husband cracked his beer and launched into the story but I wasn't listening.

The next day I sipped my coffee and watched as more people arrived. By my second cup they were lined up down the driveway like for a new blockbuster or charity turkey. I took a photo and texted it to my husband with a thumbs down emoji

and then a turd emoji too just to make my feelings crystal clear. That's when I heard the noise, a low hum really like a swarm of locusts descending through the air ducts. I held my breath and listened. It was chanting.

Chanting in the middle of day. On a street like this. I wondered if the neighbors could hear this craziness.

I knocked on the garage door but it was locked and there was no answer so, fed up, I fished the clicker off my little Jetta's visor and pressed the button not caring a goddamn what I was interrupting.

The chanting wound down and it was quiet except for the door's lurching open bit by bit, a rising curtain revealing dozens of them, more than I could count. There was Penny and I even recognized some neighbors—Don and Barbara from the realtor signs, the pot head who left her trash bins out all week, the bachelor with a perm and a hot tub—not that I socialize much.

They were sitting cross-legged or perched all over the garage's bric-a-brac like birds. They turned and squinted in my direction, shielding their eyes, faces shiny and hair dark with sweat.

I was prepared for Owen to be angry, defensive at least, that I'd interrupted their little whatever the hell it was.

But he opened his arms, revealing black pit stains, and stepped towards me with a beautiful grin.

"I've been hoping for this day."

That night my husband was sulking. Whatever the hell Owen was up to he was too busy to grill pork loins or get shit-faced at the driving range with him.

"Maybe he's trying to get his life together" is all I said.

That week I returned to the garage to listen to Owen chronicle turning his life around. He was growing out his beard and it didn't look half bad. We all clasped cold blue sodas. He had liberated cases and cases of them from his old sales job before he got the axe. I hadn't noticed what a nice voice he had before, or maybe it was the acoustics in the garage.

He sat mid-rung on an old ladder or atop a high stack of

plastic storage bins where we kept our bulky winter clothes and Christmas decorations. He referred to the garage as the place of his rebirth, motioning to the inflated kiddie pool in the corner that he slept in. Occasionally during his talks he would use something of ours to illustrate a point like when he squeezed into the rollerblades I hadn't used in years and skated round and round in circles or mounted my husband's neglected exercise bike, peddling faster and faster but going nowhere. Other times he would noodle on the Casio keyboard we bought Jonah as he talked or pick something up—an old paintball gun or dirty Halloween wig, a box of Japanese porno mags I didn't know existed—and use them as a jumping off point for the day's monologue. I felt my chest tighten every time he passed the shelf where a duct-taped hat box hid my old poetry spiral notebooks. Sometimes he trailed off and it seemed like was just snooping but then he would spin around clutching my yellowed wedding dress up to his chin and start talking about the futility of commitment in these uncertain times. How could I not be moved?

There were days he would lecture about living off the scraps of the ignorant and bourgeoisie 'zombie cows' as he wagged a scolding finger in the direction of our house (always catching my eye and giving a little shake of his head as if to say 'not you though').

We all paid the utmost attention, barely moving except to fan ourselves or wipe the sweat out of our eyes. His animated little talks (he begged us not to call them sermons) sometimes moved people to the point of passing out right on the cement flooring. If someone sneezed too much or their phone went off, Owen would blast them with our old leaf blower or toss a deflated basketball at their heads. One time Penny had the hiccups and he put her over his knee and swatted her bottom with our peeling ping pong paddle until her pale face was flush and her ailment cured.

"Bring Fireball next time if you want?" Owen said to me after a talk. Fireball is what a lot of my husband's old friends called him. But I could tell Owen didn't want him to come any

more than I did.

"He wasn't always so bad," I said to fill the silence, feeling like I should defend him a bit.

"Actually, he kind of was."

Owen and I shared a look and I realized that wry smile the first night at our dinner table wasn't too much wine or my imagination.

I excused myself to start dinner and he went to take a nap in our kiddie pool.

I wore my cutest tops to his afternoon talks and found myself sweating through them as I nodded along so vigorously that my neck ached. All the women in the garage wanted him, I suspected. Men too. At night I lay next to my sleeping husband wondering what may be happening in the inflated kiddie pool after dark. Pretty soon I was completely ignoring my deadlines for copy on a new line of doggie chew toys and press releases for an updated home orthodontics treatment. I stopped answering all work calls even though my freelancing brought in more than my husband likes to admit.

I started bringing Jonah with me to the garage and was pleased to see during Owen's speeches he didn't fidget or talk back or sneak looks at his phone or pull his hair which were all problem areas his teachers complained about. I started letting him skip school.

One day there was a loud pop like a cartoon assassination attempt. The few closest to Owen leapt up to shield him. Startled, we glanced around for the culprit. After much rummaging, Owen discovered one of our old mouse traps had been set off in the corner. We gathered around to watch as he kneeled and pulled back the metal spring. The gray animal that seconds ago was totally lifeless now twitched and bared its yellow teeth in Owen's hand. He held the creature high above his head for all in the garage to see. If there were any disbelievers among us, there weren't after that day.

"What the hell's this?" My husband found one of Owen's blue soda cans in Jonah's room. I explained they were remnants

of Owen's past life in beverage distribution in the Southwest. I didn't get into the significance. I wasn't sure I really knew the significance. Something about us helping him deplete all vestiges of his previous incarnation, sip by sip, can by can. Either way it would be lost on my husband and besides I wasn't telling him how Jonah and I were spending time in the garage.

"He doesn't want to have a drink, won't play HORSE. I texted him about making nachos and watching the game the other day and he didn't even answer!" my husband said.

I don't tell him Owen's renounced all worldly possessions. Besides the stuff we own, I mean.

"Enough is enough. He was always an odd duck," my husband said. "Time to put his ass on blast."

We were in the garage and Owen was wearing my husband's old football helmet and talking about shielding yourself against cynicism and indifference when I glanced back and saw my husband standing among the crowd by the door, half hidden behind our plastic Christmas tree. I didn't hear his Chrysler pull into the driveway and wondered how long he'd been there listening, cross-armed and open-mouthed. No doubt he came home early to put Owen's ass on blast only to find his garage full of perspiring strangers. I hoped he wouldn't make a scene but when I looked back a moment later, he was gone.

I braced myself for an earful from him that night but instead my husband ordered my favorite Chinese dumplings, enough for leftovers for days. He was adamant about us all watching a movie together and let Jonah pick. Jonah always picked *Step Brothers*, which is why my husband stopped letting him pick. But that night we watched and laughed so hard. We all know each other's favorite parts and somehow that made it funnier. After Jonah went to bed, my husband gave me a foot rub as I lay on the couch.

"I've been thinking about the garage," he said. "I'm going to convert it into a little office with a real window and cool furniture. So you have your own space. For work or just to get away and chill. Write your poetry."

I smiled appreciatively. I thought to myself the bit about my poetry is how I'll choose to remember him.

"Dan."

"Jenny," he said quietly, holding tightly onto the tops of my feet.

He knew as well as I did our garage would never be anything but a garage.

The next day Owen and I packed my Jetta and I left a note on yellow stationary for my husband on the kitchen counter. A tear stain blotted the blue ink of my signature. In the postscript I told him the refrigerator was stocked to the brim with beer, hamburger meat and all the fixings for a cook-out and not to let it go to waste. Maybe Gunner, Sully, Bobsled and whoever would keep him company. They wouldn't have to keep the stories PG and could smoke weed in the house till sunrise.

Jonah and I packed light and Owen of course had nothing besides the clothes on his back and the last couple cases of dead stock soda. He was worried about leaving his first followers but I assured him true disciples would find us eventually.

"It'll be like their first test," I said and I could tell he liked the sound of that. He squeezed my hand.

Jonah was playing with the resurrected mouse Owen had gifted him and barely glanced back as we pulled away which I took as a good sign.

We would head to a new town far away. Someplace where no one knew us and we could start again. As long as there were telephone poles to paper with flyers and a garage to preach our message.

"Maybe even a bungalow or a pool house," Owen said, stepping on the gas, eyes fixed on the horizon.

THE REVENGE APP

THE PLAN WAS TO MEET AT A COFFEE SHOP ON
Miracle Mile. He arrived early and was surprised to find her
already there and looking more or less like her photos. They
exchanged an awkward smile and an even more awkward hug.
Thank god she was the right height, more or less.

They discussed their different travel routes to get to this
coffee shop, chosen because it was more or less midway between
their residences, and then assured each other that they never,
ever did things like this i.e. used apps for dating.

Nora saw Gordon wince at the term 'dating' and she
regretted using it.

"Or whatever this is," she clarified.

She explained dating wasn't something she'd been capable
of lately either but she was trying to normalize what they were
doing, or at least planning to do.

They had both been broken up about a year. After briefly
swapping heartbreak stories and comparing emotional war
wounds, Gordon suggested they get right down to it. As per
the app's suggestion he had brought some personal effects of

Annabelle's in the trunk of his Prius. He also had multiple pages of dialogue and scenarios he'd typed up in a saved file he now felt comfortable enough forwarding to her.

Nora said she'd done the same and hoped her ex-fiancé Stevo's clothes fit him. As she spoke, Gordon held his phone close to her face to compare it with a screensaver photo of his ex, Annabelle. He was satisfied, more or less. It was as good a fit as he was going to find within the greater Los Angeles area.

Three days later they met at Gordon's apartment downtown. Nora was dressed in the black spaghetti top and capri pants Gordon gave her in the coffee shop parking lot. She'd gotten a French manicure and done the smokey-eye thing he'd had so much trouble articulating. He poured her a glass of rosé with three ice cubes and she sat on the same corner of the futon Annabelle had. Nora knew her lines too. She was good and Gordon caught himself wondering if she had any acting experience.

It all proceeded much like that night three months ago except this time when Nora got to Annabelle's part about there really being nothing more for them to say instead of Gordon countering that there was a lot more to say and that this was coming out of nowhere and they both just needed to take a step back and talk this through when they weren't so rundown and tired and besides he'd already bought their plane tickets to his cousin's wedding in Cabo and why would she do this because he was fucking crazy about her!

Instead of barreling through all that in a quivering voice and palming away salty tears while watching his girlfriend walk out the door, Gordon instead shrugged coolly, ordered Nora/Annabelle to remove her lime green panties and then had her right there on the futon.

Gordon had warned Nora that post-ravaging he would curtly ask her to leave his studio apartment, maybe even muttering something along the lines of 'don't let the door hit your ass on the way out' while he stretched out on his futon like a lion sunning itself after a big kill and clicked on the flat screen as a way to get closure. But instead Gordon improvised, holding her tight as can be for hours, muttering "I love you so much" over and over into her blonde locks smelling like the Crème de

Coco he had instructed her to shampoo with.

Nora had done such a stellar job as Annabelle that Gordon had the jitters for his debut as Stevo. He never had a nickname before and the form-fitting V-necks, gold-colored crucifix and straw boater's cap that were Stevo's "signature vibe" made Gordon uncomfortable. Plus, he was still growing out the itchy goatee Nora specified.

As planned, Nora was making patty melts for lunch when Gordon as Stevo stumbled through the front door of her Mar Vista condo while spoiling his appetite with the last bite of a Filet-o-Fish sandwich. Gordon proceeded to strut around as instructed, chewing Nicotine gum and drinking cheap port out of a ceramic mug that read "Bikini Inspector." The dialogue was challenging too. Off-color jokes, lots of railing against rampant government spending and cursing the cat. Nora would widen her eyes at him to remind him to diphthongize his vowels like Stevo's northern Wisconsin patois.

During their ensuing argument in the kitchen Gordon broke it to Nora that 'this dog won't hunt anymore' by which he meant their 8-year relationship. But before Gordon could recite any more of Stevo's folksy dialogue, Nora slapped the nicotine gum out of his port-stained mouth and kneed him in the groin. Already queasy from all the drinking and fried fish he was mildly allergic to, Gordon sunk to the peeling linoleum and sheltered his face from a storm of kicks, stomps and spit. He swallowed a mouthful of warm vomit just before Nora dropped to the floor to tug his Zubaz pants down and place him inside of her.

Driving home on the Santa Monica freeway later, Gordon proudly rated his performance an eight and his love-making a five which was fine because Nora said Stevo averaged a four. It gave him something to aim for.

For the next two weeks they crisscrossed the city, braving the traffic to visit each other's respective residences, role-playing their scenarios before plunging into spasms of intercourse that left them spent, bruised, and in Gordon's case, hyperventilating and nauseated.

Occasionally, like when Nora stubbed her toe or got her car

towed or when Gordon's condom split, they unwittingly broke character. But for the most part, they treated their dates with the utmost seriousness.

"You're the best Stevo since Stevo," Nora told him while helping him sponge off one afternoon.

She confessed that, despite what she said at their first meeting at the coffee shop, Gordon was not her first Stevo proxy. She had been on and off the app since he ended their engagement a year ago.

"One guy had the look but he couldn't do the accent. One guy had the accent and greasy skin but didn't drink enough. One guy hummed Bach when he came and Stevo would never do that."

"Wow." Gordon was taken aback.

"And one guy, I think was only pretending that he was heartbroken and that I looked like his ex. Which is such a violation." She shook her head. "It's like get on a different app, asshole."

"That's shitty. And that's not the case here," Gordon assured her.

"Oh, I know. I know," she said with a sad smile.

"Since Annabelle left there hasn't been a morning I haven't thought about dumping a bottle of painkillers in my morning Cream of Wheat. I have the bottle and everything. It's expired but I don't think that matters."

"Oh, I know honey. I know," she repeated.

Besides their first meeting that was the longest conversation they ever had as themselves.

No one was more surprised than Gordon to find himself, whilst in casual conversations or on various chat boards, recommending with an uncharacteristic enthusiasm the Revenge Fuck app. It could not, obviously, last and that was the point. There's only so many times you can cross your eyes, look down at a stranger naked except for your ex-girlfriend's discontinued Rouge Noir lipstick and scream about how you were made for each and you're never going to ever, ever let her go, before it becomes something less than cathartic. Diminishing returns

aside, Gordon had a proverbial, even literal, spring in his step maybe due to Stevo's penchant for hip-hop inspired Adidas high-tops. Gordon had adopted Stevo's outfits and habits outside his trysts with Nora and found his coworkers admiring his boater's hats and low-slung V-necks. He'd developed a taste for early morning slugs of port and a loyalty to the Wisconsin Badgers.

It wasn't long before he even found himself maybe preferring his days as Stevo with Nora more than his days as Gordon with Nora as Annabelle. But it was so hard to tell.

"Baby, how come your tartar sauce is never zingy like in these Filet-o-Fishes?!" Gordon threw open Nora's front door that afternoon like a beloved sitcom character, his lines down pat and his mastery of the accent worthy of Daniel Day-Lewis. It had been a month since that first awkward coffee and he was beginning to think his fish allergy was cured.

But instead of coming out of the kitchen with a plate of patty melts, Nora hopped up from the couch. Her hair was wild; her sundress half off. Before she could speak, a goateed man Gordon's height, build, hair color and general complexion rose up behind her like a lazy shadow.

"What in the name of fuck?" The accent was unmistakable.

Gordon barely had time to take him in—boater's hat and zebra-print Zubaz taut with erection—before the real Stevo rushed him. Gordon quickly learned Stevo was in better shape than he could ever pretend to be. Dropping the last bite of his Filet-o-Fish, Gordon was thrown against the wall, socked in the kisser and this time when he sunk to the floor no one was hopping onto him to tug down his pants and put him inside them.

Instead Stevo kicked him in the stomach with his high-top sneaker.

"I don't know what the fuck is going on but I want this joker outta here by the time I'm done pissing," he said.

Gordon struggled to his feet, his nose bleeding into his mouth. Apologizing profusely, Nora thrust a tote bag of Annabelle's clothes at him and helped him to the door.

"You poor thing. I'm sorry," Nora said. "Out of the blue, Stevo came back this morning for his favorite beer koozie and, well, we got to talking."

"Right."

"And then one thing led to another which led to sex."

"I get it."

"You were a great Stevo—heartfelt and convincing as hell! But of course, now that I have the real deal back what do I need with…" she trailed off.

"Totally understood." Gordon just wanted to get the hell out of there.

"And who knows, maybe Annabelle will come back one of these days?"

"To get her favorite koozie?" He tried and failed not to sound bitter.

"I'll leave you a great review." She hugged him, then closed the door and administered a long series of dead bolts.

Gordon stood there for a moment, blinking and bleeding in the midday sun. He wiped his bloody nose with the barely existent collar of his V-neck. The last time he had a bloody nose was on a roller-coaster with Annabelle and her family in Buena Park. He was terrified, trying to look like he wasn't but his body betrayed him. In the surprise photo taken during the ride and available as a souvenir as you exit for a jacked-up price, Annabelle and her family screamed with glee while Gordon stared zombie-like, blood escaping down his nose. Chuckling, her father had bought refrigerator magnet-sized photos for the whole family. Annabelle had laughed too.

Walking down the street looking for his Prius, Gordon realized he'd been too busy practicing dialects and drinking port to even check Annabelle's social media the two last weeks. He hadn't fantasized about ploughing his car through happy couples on the Santa Monica pier and into the Pacific Ocean once that day, maybe longer.

He tasted the blood on his lips and smiled. As for the tote bag of Annabelle's belongings, he tossed it over a chain-link fence and into a scrubby lot then broke into a wild run to avoid the temptation of retrieving it.

Instead, he took out his phone and logged back onto the app, clutching the old boater's cap to his head while he ran, lest his new accoutrement blow off.

THERE ARE NO HILLS ON THE CAPE

LILLY DIPPED A RICE CRACKER INTO THE specialty market hummus her mother had laid out on the kitchen island and wondered how much her parents knew, if anything, about her ex-boyfriend.

"This is good hummus."

"Better be. That little market is expensive."

"How was the bus?" her father asked. "Meet any wackos?"

"I had my earbuds in the whole time."

A few weeks ago, Lilly had told her mother over the phone that she and Russell had broken up. She hadn't gone into details.

"For crying out loud!" she heard her father shout after the information had been relayed. "I actually liked that one."

Russell had made a good impression over Memorial Day weekend with her parents and younger sister Danielle alike, helping with the dishes, seeming to shake every hand in a sign of peace within two rows of them at mass, dominating but not too much in Trivial Pursuit. He had the right kind of last name and was self-deprecating about the recent success of the company he co-founded—an app service that calculated the

environmental impact and social responsibility behind potential product purchases.

"Kind of like that Shazam thing but instead of telling you a song it tells you if the thing you're buying was made by kids in China or causes cancer?" her father asked, nodding approvingly.

"Exactly." Russell had flashed his winner smile.

"Very clever. Very." Her mother smiled tightly.

"He was on the approval matrix in *New York* magazine," Lilly added.

"Not me personally." Again with the smile. "Just my company."

Now summer was winding down and this weekend was supposed to be, among other things, a break from everything to do with Russell. As they stood around the kitchen island with their beverages of choice, her dad wiping the tub of hummus clean with a swoop that threatened to splinter his cracker, she scrutinized their faces trying to tell if they had Googled his name these past few weeks.

They looked old, which made her sad, but that was it.

"Want ice cream?" her mother asked. "I bought your favorite Ben & Jerry's. Chunky Monkey."

"No, no. I'm good."

"Chunky Monkey is Danielle's favorite," her father corrected her. Danielle was in her second year of medical school in Dublin and Lilly felt pretty sure she didn't know about Russell either.

"Lilly's favorite is…" Her father grabbed an envelope from the wicker basket they kept the mail in, closed his eyes and held it to his forehead. He was doing a bit Lilly couldn't place but, like most things with her father she appreciated the effort. "Peanut Butter Half-Baked?"

"Bingo!"

Was Lilly blushing? Her father always knew how to cheer her up. She hadn't been to the Cape since that time with Russell and was glad to squeeze in one more weekend before her parents closed up the old house. Her cell phone's spotty reception here put her at ease. After their last phone conversation, she had blocked Russell across all platforms but every week or so he managed to text her from a new number.

"Be that as it may." Her mother developed a formality to her voice when she felt ganged up on. "Chunky Monkey is all we have."

Lilly agreed to a bowl of ice cream, rationalizing that she was being magnanimous. She took the bowl, a sleeve of Pepperidge Farms chocolate chip cookies and another full glass of cabernet to last through whatever movie they were going to watch, into the living room. It was already late and it took a lot of scrolling to find something. Her parents weren't sure which movies they had or hadn't watched already. Her father finally suggested something with Amy Adams and her mother slurred her approval. Lilly gave a thumbs up and went to the kitchen for a refill and one last cookie. She and her therapist had set a goal for her to concentrate on her breathing and enjoy herself this weekend. For that reason, she didn't protest about how loud her mother had the volume ratcheted up or that the TV was once again on that setting that made everything look like a cheap soap opera.

Twenty minutes into the movie there was a sex scene. Lilly's cheeks grew hot. She was far too old to be uncomfortable watching a sex scene with her parents. She felt her father shift his weight on the other side of couch. It wasn't even a sex scene per se—more like a seduction, some dirty talk, frantic mutual undressing, light female nudity. She was relieved when the camera cut to inserts of scattered clothing on the tile floor the next morning.

"That actor reminds me a little bit of Russell," her mother said later.

The chiseled actor she was referring to didn't particularly look like Russell. Hadn't this actor been called out for questionable behavior with women years ago? Oh god, was her mother hinting at something? She looked at her father who acted focused on the movie. It was unclear if he hadn't heard or was just ignoring her mother because he disapproved of her chatting the whole film.

"Mom, c'mon. Enough with the talking. Seriously."

A few scenes later her mother announced that they had already watched this movie before. Her father maintained they

had not.

"Yes, we did. He goes to bed with her and then the other one gets jealous and—"

"Linda. Don't spoil it."

"Seriously, mom."

Her mother kissed her cheek with wine-soaked lips and clomped down the hall while her father sat up straight and continued watching with renewed attention. Lilly stayed where she was—even as the plot unfurled like her mother said—happy enough to take her father's side.

The next morning, she woke up late. Her father was dressed for golf and her mother was fidgeting with the espresso machine when Lilly came downstairs with wet hair from the shower.

"There she is. The Legend of Sleepy Lilly," her mother said. "If you'd gotten up earlier, I would've made you eggs but I've got errands to run."

"That's fine. I didn't want eggs. I never sleep that late." She felt defensive. "Felt good for a change."

"I bet." Her father squeezed her shoulder. "Must be nice to wake up to something other than garbage trucks and car alarms for once."

"Good burn on Brooklyn, dad."

"What are your plans for the day? You'll have to wait a bit if you want to use my car. The transmission is making a sound again so be careful on hills."

"There's like zero hills on the Cape, mom."

"Want to be my caddy? I've got two weeks before the member guest. This is the year I beat Dave fucking Krogman like a drum."

"Tom!"

"What? Fuck is not a swear. And Dave's a deadbeat cheater and a faker. Every year he brings a loudmouth ringer from New Jersey who lies about his handicap." Her father looked at her and she shrugged. "I think you played soccer with his daughter."

Lilly was used to her parents updating her on people she barely remembered. It was a small summer town.

"Do you want to use the beach club? If you want to use the

beach club, I should've called to put your name in already. You'd have to spiff up a little too."

Her mother did this thing where she would get aggressively helpful. Lilly practiced her breathing techniques.

"I just want to chill. Thanks. If I want to go to the beach, I'll go to the town beach."

"You sure?"

"Linda. Don't nag the girl. She wants to chill."

"Ok, ok. Chill away," her mother said. "I'm sure the blogging life takes a toll on you."

"Mom, you always say that. I'm not a blogger. I'm the head of social media which has literally nothing to do with blogging."

Actually, Lilly's position at the progressive athletic wear company had been downgraded to consultant and her hours trimmed back. Other coworkers had their hours cut too but Lilly couldn't help but wonder if it had anything to do with Russell. She knew her coworkers read the type of tech gossip sites that reported every sordid detail. She imagined she saw window screens minimize as she walked by their work stations. When the story first broke, she had wondered if she should make a statement and post it online, something wise and selfless that would garner all kinds of supportive comments. But she didn't get very far, unable to decide even what the appropriate app for public apologies was now.

"This isn't me nagging but I did run into Helen Wombley at the market."

"Who?"

"She said Nicole and her twins are down. You know Nicole and what's his name got divorced."

"Oh really?" Lilly couldn't help feeling a tinge of satisfaction. Lilly had silenced Nicole's Instagram account—with its perk-filled business trips to Tokyo, family ski vacations in Aspen, pole dancing workout videos—long ago.

"They were such a great looking couple. Anyway, Nicole's around if you want someone to go out with."

"I barely know Nicole."

"You've known her forever. I thought you two were pals?"

"Her parents are good people," her father added.

Lilly and Nicole were in the same sailing camp as teens. The college-aged instructors always gave Nicole special treatment. Lilly recalled a particularly humid day on a Beetle Cat as Nicole and the achingly cute instructor flirted while she struggled to man the boat, the spastic tiller bruising her ribs and the bottom of her shorts drenched with salt water. Later as she furled the sails alone, she heard Nicole tease the instructor, loud enough for her to hear, that he could've gotten a BJ if they hadn't had a third wheel.

"I just want to decompress, read my book."

Lilly performatively grabbed an orange from the bowl on the counter and headed out to the back patio so she could get a signal on her phone. Seeing there were no texts from Russell, she breathed easy and felt the day had real potential.

Lilly threw sunscreen, a towel and the books she was slowly reading—one a biography of Huey P. Newton for the book club she was determined not to skip this time, the other a book of *Paris Review* author interviews on the craft of writing—into a monogrammed tote and headed to the local beach.

The last place Lilly wanted to be was running into acquaintances and making small talk at her parents' beach club. Plus wasn't she way too old to use her parents' membership? Her mother always insisted it was fine but it made Lilly self-conscious. The public beach would be better, anonymous and she wouldn't need to 'spiff up.'

Even though it was an overcast day, she had to wait in a line of idling cars for forty minutes. When she arrived at the makeshift kiosk, a teen in medieval orthodonture told her the beach sticker on her mother's Volvo was outdated and made her turn around. Lilly drove to another beach but the lot was full. She felt so pale, she wanted at least a little sun. There was no way she could backtrack and call her mother now.

After getting turned around in yet another rotary, Lilly found herself driving past a roadside clam shack she had no doubt passed countless times over the years without a second thought. Suddenly eating there seemed like a quintessentially Cape Cod thing to do and wasn't this weekend all about having the type

of fun she had been denied all summer? She waited in a line behind a couple locals—contractors in paint-splattered pants, soft-shoe'd nurses on a lunch break maybe—and complimented herself on finding an underrated gem in plain sight. She doubted even her sister had been here.

She entertained an image of coming here with a new boyfriend next summer. She'd make sure her mother had the right beach sticker and after some sun and a swim, she'd bring him here and tell him what to order. Later he'd cite that afternoon to his friends as the moment he knew he was in love.

She ordered fried clams with bellies for the first time since she was a teenager as well as a chocolate frappé. She found a sunny corner at one of the adjacent handful of blue picnic tables and started to slug back the breaded clams one after the other, dunking them in a little paper container of chunky tartar sauce to cool them off first. The plump bellies exploded, pungent and briny, searing the roof of her mouth till her eyes watered. The frappé was so thick. She had to suck absurdly hard on the straw making her pleasantly lightheaded as she closed her eyes. A radio, probably in the kitchen, was playing that Tom Petty song that made her think of summer. Or was this Bryan Adams? Either way it all felt good, the sun finally shining on her face.

A ping noise alerted her to a text. Her lids snapped open. WHY CAN'T WE TALK THIS OVER? DON'T FREEZE ME OUT.

Immediately Lilly felt nauseated. Her hands and mouth stained with grease and bread crumbs, the frappé hardening like cold cement inside her. The phone was animated with non-stop buzzing and dings as texts poured in. With an oily hand she shoved the phone in her pocket to muffle it. She stood up quickly, felt a prick and strained to see behind her. A few blue splinters had punctured the skin below the hemline of her khakis; blood trickled down the pasty back of her thigh, bee-lining towards her white Ked slip-on. She wiped herself off but the napkins were dirty and she made more of a mess. She saw teen boys at a neighboring table, tan and shirtless in form-fitting board shorts, laughing. Did one of them just whisper *PMS*? She didn't even throw her trash in the steel drum garbage, just fast-walked her

way to the dirt parking lot, got in the Volvo, her bleeding thigh hot and sticky on the seat, and sped off.

The texts were his usual. He just wanted to talk, to explain, to correct the record. Half the things written about him weren't even true and the other half were exaggerated. None of what he did was during the time they were serious together. He already had investors interested in a podcast he was launching where he spoke with other de-platformed individuals. He didn't know what he would do if she didn't contact him.

Lilly had been down this road with him. She was surprised he was trying so hard with her. When they were together, he rarely even posted photos of the two of them online. That stung, but felt like a blessing after the allegations. Lilly was never officially name-checked as his girlfriend and hadn't replied to the one reporter's phone messages she received. There were two Getty Images of them together that one blog commenter had linked to and speculated on. "If that's his girlfriend, no wonder he was out every night hunting for strange."

Lilly didn't engage and blocked the number. Queasy from the impulsive lunch, she vomited as quietly as possible in the upstairs bathroom and took a long shower. She lay on the bed in the guest room, under the enormous crucifix that had scared her as a child, doing her morning pages and then made progress on her book about the Black Panthers. When she came downstairs, she was looking forward to a glass of merlot and helping her mother cook dinner. She wondered if her parents had seen the latest James Bond movie. She figured at least her dad would like that.

"How was the beach, sweetheart? Did you Netflix and chill?"

She was surprised to find her father, pink from the shower and in his lime green blazer. His sharp cologne filled the foyer.

"Linda!" he yelled and checked his watch.

"You're leaving?"

"The Goodmans are having their end-of-summer cocktail thing," her mother said, hurrying down the hall in white jeans that were too tight, struggling to clasp a seashell bracelet to her

wrist. "I said that last night."

"No, you didn't."

"Well the hideous invitation is right on the fridge. Besides we figured you were going out with Kelly or Jen?"

"What? I haven't seen Kelly or Jen in years."

"Ok, ok. We just figured you wouldn't want to hang out with us old farts again."

"That's the whole reason I came here."

"Why don't you come with us?" her father proposed. "The Goodmans put out quite a spread. Last year they had an oyster bar. A guy with an earring played Jimmy Buffett songs."

"Actually, I don't think kids are allowed." Her mother was addressing her father. "You know how Diane is about RSVPs."

"I'm hardly a kid." Lilly felt like she needed to make this point even though there was no way she was going to third wheel it with her parents to a cocktail party.

"The Goodmans are RSVP Nazis." her father conceded. "Why don't we all just stay in then?"

"Tom. Do you have any idea how long I just spent getting ready?"

"No, no, no. You guys are going," Lilly said.

The only thing more pathetic than tagging along would be guilt-tripping them to stay home. "Please. I just want to watch a movie anyway. Maybe the new Bond," she added for her father's benefit.

"Now I don't want to go. That new Bond's really grown on me," her father said.

Lilly theatrically ushered them out.

"Have fun storming the castle!" she called after them, waving.

Her mother gave the tight smile she gave when she didn't understand something but her father laughed at the reference.

She was sad to see them go which made her feel even more pathetic but at least now she was positive they didn't know about Russell. They wouldn't have left her alone like this otherwise.

Before her father's convertible was even out of the driveway, Lilly was on the couch with a glass of wine, eating her way through a Tupperware container of overly-dressed pasta salad.

Her parents had a lot of channels. Maybe she'd watch one of the Criterion movies she'd been meaning to cross off her list. Was it Truffaut or Godard she liked? There were four remote controls of varying size lined up on the end table and a fifth protruding from between the couch cushions.

Ten minutes later, Lilly was still mashing buttons on various remotes, struggling to actually turn the television on when her phone vibrated against the thick glass of the coffee table. She could make out that it was an unknown number.

Without picking it up, she leaned over her phone squeamishly as if checking a rat trap.

HEY BITCH! DRINK?...
THIS IS NICOLE WOMBLEY BTW

Lilly agreed over text to meet Nicole out for one drink at Spinnakers. She put her hair in a ponytail, threw on a windbreaker and borrowed her mother's Volvo again. The transmission was making a bit of a weird sound.

Lilly figured Nicole must be desperate if she was resorting to texting her. Her husband must have gotten the friends in the divorce. Lilly didn't want to go for drinks with anyone too fulfilled right now. Being an ear to bend was as much as she was up for. Plus she was confident Nicole was too absorbed with her own busy life to have clocked anything, like Russell, happening in Lilly's.

There were only two places to get a drink in town. The grill room at the dusty surf n' turf restaurant on main street or the little bar at the marina. Lilly dreaded running into people she knew at both. She chose Spinnakers hoping it might be less crowded but it was standing room only when she squeezed her way inside.

The crowd was as constant as the faded buoys and framed limericks adorning the walls. The Series 7 set in customized fleece vests and flip-flops, middle-aged men's faces flushed as their Nantucket reds, pounding gin n' tonics with one eye on the baseball game, the women in sailor striped tunics or preppie pastels texting to check on the babysitter. But for the most part it was a younger crowd, baseball hats and college sweatshirts

frayed at the collar; fresh-faced yacht crew members in polos emblazoned with boat names blowing off steam. There was a sloppy frat house din to the place.

She spotted Nicole being mooned over by a bartender. She was wearing a form-fitting floral romper that showed off her long legs. Her hair looked amazing. Lilly felt like a slob, her hair a greasy rat's nest, and was about to turn on her heel when Nicole spotted her and waved for the college kids at the bar to squeeze down.

"Lilly! God you never change. Got you a Seabreeze."

She thrust a plastic cup in her hand; the fruity cocktail sloshed over her fingers.

"You look amazing," Lilly told her.

"What?!" she answered but Lilly was sure she heard her.

"Great to see you! It's been a minute!"

"You doing alright? My mom said your mom said you had a break-up."

Damn it. Her mother never missed a chance to cast her as a victim and now Nicole had beaten her to the punch. At least Nicole didn't seem to know more than that. Lilly tried to laugh it off but her laugh sounded nasal, more like a honk.

"That was nothing really. A conscious decoupling as Gwyneth would say." What the fuck was she blathering about? She switched gears, lowered her voice. "But what about you? I heard about you and Peter. Now that's hard."

"Actually, it was a relief. I got two kids out of it and the moment word was out literally every single friend of his was trying to fuck me and he knows it." Nicole shrugged. "Which is almost better than sex."

"Wow." Lilly tried to sound encouraging but with a hint of concerned skepticism. "You've landed on your feet?"

"My mom thought she saw you eating at that random clam shack by the rotary? My kids always want to go there. Is that place even sanitary?"

Small fucking town. Lilly shuddered to think what she looked like alone and bingeing clams by the fistful earlier. It was now painfully clear Nicole had reached out to her out of pity.

"To swinging single," Lilly said, blowing past Nicole's

comment and holding up her cup to toast. She was being ironic but that was lost in the bar's clamor and the line rung in her ears like bad romcom dialogue.

They touched plastic cups and drank. Nicole was looking past her.

"I actually see the new tennis pro over there. Sven. He's hilarious. Have you taken a lesson with him?"

"Oh? No. Can you take lessons using your parents' membership still?"

Nicole focused on her like she was seeing her for the first time. "Of course not. I use my own membership."

"Right. Yeah. I knew that." God, Lilly wished she was on her parents' couch watching a French film, anything but this. She took a long sip to save herself from having to speak.

"Sven's putting on his jacket. I'm gonna grab him before he leaves. I'll bring him back. You're ok here for a second, right?"

Nicole didn't wait for her answer. She squeezed across the bar, turning heads and tossing out waves like she was running for office, before heading off her quarry. He couldn't have been more than 27 or 28, Lilly thought. He was more than happy to post up with her by the scuffed-up jukebox. Nicole wasn't coming back anytime soon. Lilly finished her drink and then downed Nicole's too.

She tried to flag the bartender repeatedly. When he finally did walk towards her it was to serve the older man next to her.

"The usual and whatever this young lady is having."

It took Lilly a moment to realize he was referring to her.

"Oh? A Seabreeze please," she stammered, embarrassed by the inadvertent rhyme. She may as well stick with what Nicole had thrust in her hand.

The bartender hopped to it.

"Thank you," she said.

The man was probably a few years younger than her father, bulkier and squatter. Gray chest hair burst from the openings of his misbuttoned and untucked Oxford and it was hard to tell the spills from sweat stains. His barrel chest was probably attractive once but now competed for prominence with his belly, like a camel's double hump.

"I think I know those freckles. Are you a Maddock?"

"Oh yes. Lilly." Lilly didn't like being identified but it couldn't be helped. She had her father's features. "Hi."

"Ah yeah. Lilly the writer."

It had been so long since she'd heard herself described that way she thought for a minute he was mistaking her for someone else.

"Dave Krogman." He smiled even as he talked. "Friend of your parents. I remember being over for drinks one night and you were heading off to celebrate with friends. Your story was going to be in *The New Yorker* or something?"

"Oh jeez. Definitely not *The New Yorker*." Lilly imagined herself, probably in one of her tailored indie band t-shirts and black jeans, bubbly and talking herself up to her parents' friends as she headed out the door; desirable, full of potential.

"Must've been the time I got into my college lit mag?"

"Regardless, I was impressed."

"Good memory."

"Ever since I started beating him in golf, your father never has me over to the house anymore."

Now Lilly remembered the name. Always Dave fucking Krogman according to her father.

"It's hard for me to imagine anyone taking golf so seriously."

"My feelings exactly."

He polished his smudged tortoise shell glasses with his shirt tail, giving her a peek at his swollen belly. He was bursting out of his madras shorts.

The drinks came. He and the young bartender exchanged a joke she didn't quite catch.

"Thanks again for the drink."

"Of course. They know me well here," he said unprompted. "I've been staying on the Hold My Calls all month."

"Excuse me?"

He motioned towards the docks. "That's my sailboat."

She followed his gaze out the dark window. "That sounds like a fun way to spend the summer."

"That's debatable. When you're in a marital spat, it's better than staying in the dog house," he said. "But you're too young to

know about all that."

"Keep cleaning your glasses. Nearly all my friends are married. With kids."

"Well there's no rush. My daughter Ali just had her first one."

"I remember Ali. I think I'm older than her."

"Really?" He sucked on his capped teeth, looking her up and down. "Hard to believe."

"I should get back to my friend." She craned her neck, hoping to get Nicole's attention.

"Stop by the boat anytime if you want to go for a sail. Or have a nightcap on the deck."

Now that she was moving away, he was staring right at her chest. "Second to the last slip on the right. Hold My Calls."

She smiled politely and made her way over to where Nicole and Sven were talking, motioning to the other end of the bar.

"Can you believe that guy creeping on me? Almost my dad's age. Like no thank you."

When Lilly realized Nicole and Sven either didn't hear her or were just ignoring her, she pretended like she had a call, clasped her phone to her ear and walked out of the bar and to the car.

The kitchen lights were still on. That was typical of her mother who didn't even recycle. Lilly walked in the back entrance and swung opened the refrigerator door. She took out a plastic tub of leftover spaghetti Bolognese and jumbo bag of Cape Cod potato chips. Planning to top it all off with some Advil, she reasoned that carb loading would help stifle a potential hangover.

"Hello police, I'd like to report a hamburglar."

Lilly caught the scream in her throat and spun around.

"Dad! You scared the hell out of me."

"*If you're fond of sand dunes and salty air. Quaint little villages here and there. You're sure to fall in love with old Cape Cod,*" her father crooned. "Remember that one?"

"Definitely not."

She stood there, hugging the assortment of snack food. She imagined how ridiculous she must look. Meanwhile, even glassy-eyed with his silver hair mussed and shirt rumpled her father still looked straight out of an old Rat Pack photo.

"Grab me one of those fruity waters, will you?" He sidled up to the kitchen island. "So I guess your quiet night at home didn't last long?"

Lilly quickly put back the spaghetti and brought the chips, two cans of cran-raspberry flavored sparkling water and glasses with ice over. She liked this tableau, father and daughter catching up in the kitchen. She tried to appear as sober as possible considering she drove her mom's Volvo home.

"Nicole texted me randomly. Wanted to meet for a drink."

"The Grill Room?"

"Spinnakers."

"Ah," her father nodded. "Crowded?"

"Yeah. I saw your golf pal. Dave."

"Oh, fuck that cheapskate." Her father made a sour face. "He's a cheating asshole. I have a half a mind to petition the club to revoke his membership. But first I'm going to beat his ass in two weeks. What was he doing there?"

"Just standing around drinking like everyone else."

"Nicole back on her feet?"

"I'll say," Lilly said.

"Good for her. She was always a firecracker."

"I mean yeah she's putting on a good show." Lilly cleared her throat. "But you can tell she's in rough shape. Not a happy camper that's for sure."

"That's too bad." Her father didn't sound convinced. He was just sitting there, watching her eat chips. Was she acting really drunk? She removed her hand from the bag.

"You know," he started. Oh god, she was going to get a lecture about driving drunk.

"Russell contacted me."

Her breath hitched. She realized she was drunk as she hadn't thought about Russell since she left the bar. She wanted this conversation terminated as quickly as possible.

"When? He shouldn't be contacting you." The anger she'd

had for Russell paled compared to what she felt now.

"We used to play Words with Friends so he messaged me. Said you were having issues at work. Said you weren't returning his calls."

"Yes, because we broke up. I like a clean break." She tried to sound in control. "He clearly didn't tell you what really happened."

She didn't mean to say that last part but she was so flustered, so mad. She didn't want her father to know what happened. That was the whole point. Before she could clarify, he spoke.

"He told me what happened."

"Did he?" She would kill Russell. "I can guarantee he didn't tell you everything."

"Of course. You're right." Her father nodded. "So your mother and I Googled it."

Lilly put her hands on the kitchen island's cool granite and practiced her breathing. The idea of her father reading the snarky articles with the vivid descriptions, email transcripts and snippets of late night texts was too much. Plus, there was the comments section.

"Really awful stuff." He was being understated to spare her. "Just awful."

Lilly stared into her pink flavored sparkling water, wanting to disappear in the bubbles.

"Yeah, I'm fine though, dad. I'm seeing a therapist type-person. I'm fine."

She mustered a brave toothless smile to assure him. She wanted to give him permission to never bring this up again. He nodded back and she clamped a plastic clip on the bag of chips to signal she was about to go to bed.

"The thing is your mom and I don't want to see you throw the baby out with the bathwater."

She froze.

"When your mom met me, I was no great shakes. Granted that was a different time."

Lilly was sure she was going to throw up. To steady herself she met her father's gaze the way you focus on the horizon line when you're seasick.

"You're saying you want me to go out with Russell again?"

"I'm just saying life moves fast. We don't want you to end up, you know, unhappy."

Lilly stood there, blinking.

Her father kissed her on the head and made his way off to bed. In a daze, she unfurled the bag of chips, her crunching amplified in the empty kitchen.

Her hands are slick from the chips as she gets in her mother's Volvo and slams the door hard. She definitely shouldn't be driving. But it's only a couple miles back to the marina.

She imagines the wet chill of the wind blowing the hair across her face as she strides across the dark water, hulls on either side of her rocking like cradles with the chop, the creak of the dock below her feet, announcing her arrival.

Hold My Calls. Second slip before the end.

Taking advantage of the empty road, she drives fast and turns up the radio on a Fleetwood Mac song. Or is this Steely Dan. She's really flying now.

She hasn't thought far enough in advance to know what she will do when she gets on the boat.

But she knows she'll stay until morning and only leave when the marina is bustling with people. Small summer town and all.

NON-ESSENTIAL WORKERS

IN THIS ONE DREAM I'M WEARING A SCUZZY PINK bathrobe and convinced my one-eyed cat Jinx has the virus and will sputter out in my arms soon like a broken toy, leaving me alone with thoughts of my dead husband's Magnum gathering dust atop the credenza.

But I don't have a cat named Jinx or a dead husband. I have a high-maintenance Weiner dog with glaucoma named Gravy and an immunocompromised millennial girlfriend chanting in the living room. Lately she keeps asking me to meditate with her, to clear my mind.

"What's a credenza?" I ask from the doorway.

"Ahhhhhm," she says. "Ahhhhm."

There's a reoccurring dream where I'm among a throng of masked protestors but no one understands my cardboard sign (including me).

In another dream I'm living in a tattered tent on a hot concrete median. The tent shimmies with every passing car and the exhaust fumes make me dizzy. I recognize the guy who fishes through our recycling bins on Tuesdays snoring in a cartoon

113

sleeping bag next to me.

Then there's the dream where I'm talking with my father over FaceTime. He's in the hospital. But he's definitely not my father. I only understand bits of the Spanish we're speaking. He coughs and clutches rosary beads in his calloused hand. The connection is spotty and the masked nurse has trouble working the iPad.

"You never tell me about your dreams," my girlfriend Maya says when I tell her about all this. She sounds tickled like this is a benchmark for us.

"Let's not make a big deal."

But she's already made room for me on the couch and hit pause on her laptop. I sit down with a bottle of Bavarian dark lager.

"People's dreams suck. Nobody wants to hear about them."

"I do."

"You are the exception to the rule, babe."

"This is such great serendipity cause Ram Dass actually talks a lot about dreams."

She spins the laptop around to show me a frail old man paused, mid-profundity no doubt, poolside, a lush Hawaiian backdrop behind him.

"He says what we call dreams are actually just experiences we're having on other, non-physical planes."

"And that's his house? I'm in the wrong business."

"I'm sending you a link," she says.

Maya's been journaling and listening to whale sounds, ordering crystals and watching a lot of New Age lectures on YouTube lately; going down some wellness rabbit hole.

There are worse pandemic hobbies, I guess.

She keeps saying I need a hobby, especially now, to which I always hold up one of my beer of the month club bottles or point to *Jeopardy* on TV.

"The weird thing is some people I know are in the dreams," I explain to her. "But not people I know-know. Like the young guy with problem skin who lives with his mom in 3B, he watches seriously disturbing porn. Marco the dog walker. Last night I was in a sleeping bag next to that homeless guy who picks

through our bins."

"Poor Marco," she says. "I feel bad for him."

"I'm not paying someone to walk this dog when we're trapped at home all day and can do it ourselves."

"Marco's a professional. Plus, there's the camaraderie."

"C'mon. He gets high and hangs out with other people's pets all day." We've been through this. "Camaraderie? This dog hates other dogs."

"This must be killing his business. He was just about to incorporate. What's he doing in the dream?"

"Just you know, Marco stuff. Walking dogs."

I don't tell her the dream with Marco splashing me. The two of us are swimming in a blue lake somewhere. It's pretty. The remnants of a picnic sit on the grassy bank. He gets out of the lake and I see he's naked. He has a mandala tattoo on one shoulder and all that dog walking has kept him in good shape. Then he is standing on the big knot of a frayed rope swing, sailing in an arc far overheard as he eclipses the sun with a goofy smile and prepares to cannonball down next to me.

"The thing is I'm not me in the dreams." I take a big swill of bitter beer. "I'm another person."

Maya narrows her eyes like now we're getting somewhere. "Who are you?"

"I'm different people. Like in the dream with the one-eyed cat I'm upset about the cat getting the virus because I read some bullshit post on Facebook."

"Cats can get it?"

"No. Chances are next to nothing a house cat can get it. I got up and researched it online in real life but in the dreams, I'm still freaking out and paranoid."

"That is really weird," she agrees. "Cause you hate cats."

"I don't hate cats. I'm allergic."

"And you deactivated Facebook."

"I know!" I shout louder than I mean to. I feel like she's losing the thread of the conversation. "I'm only on Facebook in my dreams. My dreams aren't just weird. They're not mine."

"Don't they say you're everyone in your dreams?"

"Not in this case. Trust me."

"Matthew McConaughey was on Marc Maron's podcast saying he had a nocturnal emission dream that he was floating down the Amazon. The next day he bought a plane ticket to go to Peru for six months."

"Nice to be him."

Maya twists her mouth like she's deciding what toppings she wants on her pizza. "You should start writing down the dreams on index cards and then matching them with all the people whose dreams you could be having."

"Like a serial killer board? But I don't even know who the suspects are?"

"Wait I've got it! You know what you need to do in one of these dreams." She sits up straight. "Look in a mirror."

"Babe. If I had control of these dreams would I be petting a cat with my allergies or sweating my ass off at a protest?"

I don't even broach how I would definitely not be skinny-dipping with our weirdly buff dog walker.

"All right. I didn't realize you were mister dream expert."

"No, I'd be grabbing a steak somewhere or going to a movie."

She unfolds the laptop and goes back to the old man in Hawaii talking about welcoming death. I sip my beer slowly.

"My jaw is sore," I say.

"From what?"

"Clenching it in my sleep"

That night I dream my cat is sick, the lake is cold, the tent hot and the Latino man is coughing over FaceTime. I wake up drenched and twitchy, make coffee, put on my dumb mask and walk our goofy little dog even though it's still dark. He's too blind to know the difference. We walk the same eight block loop twice a day, passing the same shuttered shops and makeshift encampments. This is our whole world now.

I never put much stock in dreams, or reality. But with me having other people's dreams, I can't help but wonder if anyone is having mine. There were anxiety dreams where I had slipped up and was drinking again—like really drinking—or stranded in white-knuckle traffic on the 405, late for some big something. Good riddance to those. But there were good dreams too like

that one with the flirty redhead from my office or others where Alex Trebek showed up and we spoke in "answers in the form of a question." I never miss *Jeopardy* plus he's battling the same type of cancer my dad lost to years ago. If whoever's having my dreams is lucky, they'll have one where I'm playing drums with my old garage band. Or the recurring one where I'm riding on the back of my dad's Harley on a fall day, my stomach full with pancakes or a roadside cheeseburger, my skinny kid arms goose-pimpled and barely long enough to wrap around his waist, not wanting our one weekend a month to end, the foliage like blurred rainbows flanking me. We got along best going 80 miles per hour, my face pressed against his broad back.

God, I loved being on that bike.

Even though they were mostly nonsense, I miss my own dreams. Maybe Maya's right and I should order some index cards and a bulletin board. Passing under a street lamp, I eye my long shadow and imagine myself some kind of dream detective, hot on the case.

Days, or is it weeks, later, we're scrolling looking for a show or movie we can agree on. Smoke from a ring of fires around the city blurs the sun during the day and the summer heat sets records causing palm trees to burst into flames like tiki torches. The sunset cheering for first responders and essential workers has petered out, replaced by the all-night hiss and bang of illegal fireworks lit not to celebrate but provoke. The dog howls along with the parade of passing ambulances. The city has lowered air quality regulations to allow for more cremations. I read someone on Twitter joke that's why we have such great sunsets lately.

Maya's putting on weight and I assume she's noticing the same about me. The flesh under my eyes is dark and puffy and during endless Zoom meetings my coworkers direct message me to ask if I'm okay. Not the redhead though but probably better that way. Luckily, I can nod off and still not miss anything about next quarter's sales enablement strategies. No one would mistake us for essential workers, that's for sure.

"Remember that podcast I told you to listen to?"

I nod. Maya is always recommending books and podcasts now. Usually there's some spiritual bent or something about how white people suck. I wish she could just take up baking bread like her friends.

"I was just listening to today's episode and it made me think of your dreams.

"That's just it. They're not my dreams—"

"I know, know. The host was talking about how the quarantine has silenced so much of our frivolous behavior that it's turning the volume up on what's really important," Maya says. "The same way blind people have a much better sense of smell."

"All right." I take the bait. "But how does that explain me dreaming about the freaking dog walker or someone else's dad?"

I'm being a jerk because I wake up every morning feeling like a TV that's been left on all night playing static, my wires crossed and sparking. I'm sick of shutting my eyes and seeing strangers projected on a loop. I want to unsubscribe, unfollow whatever this is.

"You're dreaming other people's dreams, right. Maybe," Maya draws the word out. "You miss them."

She's scrolling through a delivery app. Pizza. Salads. Thai, the poke bowls place. We're not only running out of shows to watch, we're low on reasonable places to order from. I'm annoyed she's going through dinner options while we're still looking for a show.

"Who?"

"The people in your dreams. People in general. Everyone."

"What's that supposed to mean?"

"Maybe you miss all those day to day interactions. Seeing faces. Trading smiles. Connecting." I can tell she thinks she's being insightful. "That's the kind of stuff that makes us feel normal."

"How can I miss any of these people? I don't even know their names."

I kind of know what Maya's getting at. We did couples counseling once on account of her accusing me of being 'closed off' and not having enough 'outlets.' At the end of the hour the

therapist said I used humor as a defense mechanism. "What an amazing insight," I complimented him. "You just cracked the case." We didn't go back. Not long after I sensed which way the wind was blowing and cut out drinking everything but beer. You can only get in so much trouble with beer.

"I mean I know I miss people, even the ones I don't really know," Maya is still talking. "I miss small talk. I miss interacting. That and going out for sushi. You should get on one of the neighborhood apps, get involved. Someone just started a GoFundMe for a community fridge."

"Maybe."

I was never Mr. Small Talk. No one ever mistook me for a people person. I always tell Maya it's generational; my reluctance to socialize is part of the Gen X chill she loves about me.

"Maybe all these changes are opening you up, getting you more in tune with, I dunno, other people's vibrations."

"Is this you or Ram Dass talking?"

"Have you watched any of the links I emailed you?"

"Maybe all your meditation and Tarot cards and New Age books have put some voodoo on me. You've opened up some weird portal."

"I don't even read Tarot. Honestly, I wish you'd watch some of those links. If the salon doesn't open back up soon, I may go back to school for energy work. Glendale has one of the best Reiki institutes."

"Maybe you're the one who should be getting these transmissions, not me."

"I can't tell if you're kidding or not right now," she says.

"I'm just tired is all."

"I have my own dreams," she says pointedly.

To prove how full her dream dance card is she describes one she had last night. It's something about us at her favorite sushi restaurant. At least I'm in it. I'm wearing this navy sweater she gave me last Christmas and being very affectionate, even holding her hand in public, then I reveal I booked us tickets to this resort in Kauai her sister went to.

I get the sense this is dream is bullshit and tell her to pull the trigger on dinner and that I'm going to walk our goofy little

dog.

I do the usual eight block loop with the dog, same everything like living in a fish bowl. Not only is the dog losing his sight, now he's getting fat too. Maybe I need to walk a little farther.

I actually don't mind wearing the mask. I walk in the middle of the street and it's so quiet I can hear all the TVs inside the living rooms like the ugly houses flanking me are trading secrets. A spindly coyote hobbles past and I pull the dog close. I hear a car alarm in the distance, then another. Everyone's getting the catalytic convertors sawed out of their Priuses lately.

I pass a shirtless man picking through black garbage bins but it's not my guy.

I exchange nods with a Latino man my age walking with a decayed soccer ball under one arm. Man, he looks drained. I wonder if he's the man with the sick father and the bad FaceTime connection. I half-heartedly think maybe I could say something helpful or tell him not to hold back with his old man if only my Spanish was better. I can barely order dinner in Rosarito. He glances at me and I look away.

I'm half a block away from our building when I see an older woman dragging her garbage bins down to the curb. Her hair's splayed everywhere like she just got tossed from a moving car. She's not familiar but as she passes under the street lamp her scuzzy pink bathrobe is. I recognize the coffee-stained sleeves from the dreams where I'm nursing a tall glass of vodka and petting the one-eyed cat, sick with worry about the little guy. Even the off-brand vodka bottles I spot piled high in the recycling bin seem familiar.

I remember the gun on her credenza.

"Jinx is gonna be ok," I blurt out.

It's muffled cause I have my mask on.

She doesn't hear me and is staggering back up the driveway. I feel silly saying it louder. But I should act, like Matthew McConaughey flying to Peru.

I tug my mask down and clear my throat to speak again but her front door has already clicked shut. I spot the cat watching me with his one good eye from the windowsill before I turn

away.

"Fuck it," I say to myself.

When I walk back inside our apartment there's an incense candle burning and Maya is on the phone. She seems buoyant in a way she isn't with me lately. Sometimes we don't even say hello when we pass each other in the hall during the days.

She cups the phone. "Poke bowls are on the way."

I'm regretting not saying something earlier, because that was my least favorite of the dinner options, when there's a knock. Usually when I open the door, the delivery person has their back towards me, retreating briskly down the exterior walkway.

No contact drop-off is the new normal and I'm not complaining.

Tonight, I find the plastic bag at my feet but the lanky delivery guy is still there. Between his restaurant logo'd mask and tired eyes are the same inky purple bags I have. For a moment I think he's waiting for a tip but of course that's all done on the phone.

He's staring at me like he knows me. Then I realize it.

"Hold it." I snap my fingers, feeling more animated than I've been in weeks. "Do you know me? Like recognize me?"

He stands there, blinking.

"Did you ride the motorcycle? The fall colors back east, right?! There's nothing like it! That's my dad driving, you know?"

I'm excited, like I'm meeting the only other person in the world that's heard my favorite song. I must seem way too eager because the delivery guy retreats and fast. He nearly bumps into the mama's boy with rosacea from 3B as he hurries down the stairs and to his Datsun double-parked in the lot below.

"You dreamt about the old band, right!? Playing drums? Alex Trebek!?" I shout, leaning so far over our first floor railing I have to catch myself.

But he's already driving away.

I straighten up and look around, winded and suddenly self-conscious about the neighbors hearing me. The guy with blotchy skin who watches demented porn is staring at me from the other side of his smudged apartment window now. His mask

is still attached to his ears but pulled down around his lack of a chin. He looks freaked out and I can't blame him, panting from his little brush with humanity on the steps. I see his mother's hunched shadow on the wall behind him. What a life. I wonder how many years Maya and I have lived a few units down from them.

"We've never really met." I give the most innocuous wave I can. "I'm Marty."

"Philip."

I stand there for a moment, nodding like an idiot. "What a crazy time to be alive, Philip."

"Were you just yelling at the delivery guy?" Maya muffles the phone again when I walk back in.

"What? No." I say. "Our incel neighbor."

"Who?"

"With the jammy skin? When this is all over maybe you know someone to fix him up with?"

Not seeing that I'm being sincere, Maya waves me away and goes back to her call.

I wash my hands and open a beer, thinking how overboard I went with the delivery guy. He was probably freaked out that some lunatic with no mask was chasing after him. He probably didn't recognize me at all. If he did, I hope it wasn't from anything weird I was doing in my own dreams. Now we'll have to order goddamn poke again just so I can explain myself to the guy.

Maybe Maya was onto something about me. I should dust off my Spanish skills at least, try again with the cat lady down the street. I squeeze her shoulder as I pass but she doesn't register it. She's giggling and I can tell she's talking to her sister, making private little jokes and later loudly regretting the fact she won't be able to see her and visit their uncle's lake house in Oregon this summer.

"I love that lake so much," I hear her say more than once before she hangs up.

We settle into our spots on the couch and unpack the takeout bag with a couple poke bowls and chopsticks. I drink a bottle of amber ale with a burnt toffee aftertaste and scroll through shows

with the remote: serial killer show, Tiger King, the new Michael Jordan thing, cheap Netflix comedy, Jeffrey Epstein series, more cult stuff. I wish *Jeopardy* was on but apparently it's the weekend.

"You should Venmo the dog walker for a few walks just to be nice." Maya fumbles with the chopsticks and a clump of poke falls to the carpet where the dog snatches it up. "Marco could probably use the help. Poor guy."

My scrolling slows down and then comes to a halt. Maya looks over at me with a big mouthful of rice and fish.

Then I put the beer down and gulp hard, take out my phone and do just as she asked me to. In fact, I send him an absurd amount of money and then I continue scrolling.

I can only hope whoever is having my dreams is as charitable during these trying times.

THE FOODIE DETECTIVE

PART I

I'm perched on my usual stool at the bar, finishing a spicy michelada and my latest review when I feel eyes on me. A few stools down a brunette, no make-up per se and hair pulled back brutally tight, side-eyes me over her margarita's salted rim. Despite her best efforts, I still smell money. A natural beauty. No wedding ring.

She stands out in the Boyle Heights crowd at Los Toros Cantina. Me, I've had enough practice to blend in; I may as well be another dusty sombrero on the wall or dying fern.

"Are you…" she pauses hoping I'll finish for her. But I don't. "… Mr. Mustard?"

I drain my massive drink by way of an answer, paw the rim's tamarind sauce from mouth. I make a show of snapping my battered laptop shut. My latest food column, *To Live and Dine in LA*, is already a day late but that's early for me.

"Want to split a plate of molotes?"

She shrugs. In my line of work, it's rare to have someone to

125

share with and my waistline is reflecting that. I sit up straight and motion to Xavier, my old friend and the place's swizzle stick-chewing owner. He knows exactly what I want; that's how often I'm here.

Over fried appetizers and another round of drinks, Tatiana tells me she works for a group called Animals First. I understand now why she's dressed like a communist and not touching the little chorizo-filled bombs I'm baptizing in salsa verde and shoveling away. So much for sharing.

I nod like I've heard of the group. My ex, Mandy, is also vegan. When I met her we would road trip to Tijuana just for our favorite adobada tacos, be first in line Sunday mornings for Roscoe's Chicken n' Waffles and save up all summer for dinner at Chez Panisse. Later she cut out beef, then fish, then dairy... then me.

"My group has gotten reports about these new underground dinners in LA. Off menu, black-market dishes. Whale, horse, you name it," she explains. "I heard you may be able to find the person behind this; that you know the city better than anyone."

"The culinary corners of it maybe," I say modestly. "What happens if I find this person?"

"Contact me. We'll do the rest."

She sees I'm waiting for more.

"Citizen's arrest for a misdemeanor," she clarifies. She smiles and it's showstopping enough for me to vow not to eat that last juicy molote. "We're vegans, not vigilantes."

"There's crossover. Just ask my ex." As both a stab at humor and way to let her know I'm single, the comment falls flat.

"So. Can you help?"

"Maybe."

I mean it to sound mysterious but I'm thinking. If there's anything I've learned in my handful of cases it's to keep expectations as low as possible.

My new side-hustle was born a couple months ago after a green-haired woman starting screaming. From my stool at Los Toros, I saw her pointing to a guy hunched over in the corner red booth with blood streaming from his mouth. Seems

a piece of glass made it into his chilaquiles. Most people were too busy watching the Dodgers game to notice. Knowing better restaurants have gone under for less, Xavier cleaned him up and gave him nearly a grand out of the till to keep quiet.

I ended up following him when he left. Maybe I had a hunch or needed to stretch my legs or was thinking of Mandy's parting shot out the door about me watching and scribbling, but never doing, as the world passed me by. First, I tailed him to the liquor store where he bought a new t-shirt and a tall boy of beer and then to the best hot chicken joint on this side of the city where he pulled the exact same routine. But this time I snapped his photo with my phone which we ran with my next column. That column got a huge reader response from owners bamboozled by the phony glass eater and my nom de plume, Mr. Mustard, earned a reputation as a go-to gastronome for help with, for lack of a better term, culinary criminals. A foodie fixer if you will. And because Xavier likes to brag to anyone who'll listen that Mr. Mustard uses his hole in the wall restaurant's bar as a de facto office, those in need knew right where to find me.

An owner with a thieving waitstaff, a restauranteur who needs a sober companion for his wild card chef, a fried chicken magnet who thinks his family recipe's been stolen; the desperate people pilgrimaging my way run the gamut and that they actually believe I could help them is a much needed ego boost. But Tatiana's the first client I'm tempted to give a discount to because she reminds me of the ex. That resemblance also makes me want to charge her double.

I split the difference and tell her my fee plus expenses and say I prefer Venmo. She tucks five hundred-dollar bills along with her number on a napkin under my michelada, tells me to text as soon as I'm close and slides off her stool.

"We'll be in touch!" I feel compelled to yell as she crosses off and casts a confused look back at me. I wave off my own dumb comment.

I'm still very much a food writer first, food detective second.

Xavier, polishing a glass in eavesdropping distance, isn't shy about his eyes tracking her out the door. His place, his rules he likes

to say. We went to Catholic school together and even then, he gave the young nuns hell.

He strolls towards me clucking his tongue. Handsome and flirty, Xavier's used to being the center of attention when there's a pretty woman in his family's establishment.

"Aren't you Mr. Popular lately?"

"You know of any underground dinners going on where they serve exotic fare. Whale, that kind of thing?"

"Too rich for my blood. Chapulines in my tacos is as crazy as I get."

"Hmm." Now that she's gone, I gobble the last greasy molote.

"Considering you use my place as your office, you should really give me a cut of your fee," he says. "Hell, I'm practically your agent."

"Add it to my tab." I rattle the chili powder-dusted cubes in my glass for another michelada and stifle a hot greasy burp. I feel a flare-up in my chest and fish into the pocket of my army jacket for a couple Pepto tablets. I'm sweating and lumber off to the restroom.

"Mr. Mustard is on the case," Xavier laughs, making my drink.

PART II

The city is awash in pop-ups, illegal restaurants and underground dinners. Lately it seems there's more underground than above. I scroll a dozen online food boards looking for any mention of illegal edibles like kujira or shark.

I crisscross the city talking up contacts. A taco slinger in Lincoln Heights turns me onto to his aunt's Monday night goat dinners in her co-op. A Glendale bar-back invites me to a queer Persian supper club after hours at a Knights of Columbus. A sous chef hips me to an aphrodisiac-heavy tasting menu and cuddle party every full moon in Woodland Hills.

My editor Suki Fleck at *The LA Beat* scoffs and tells me she's heard rumors of endangered species dinners for years.

"It's the foodie equivalent of Big Foot," she says. "Forget that. I want you to write up the new gastropub thing in the Arts District."

Despite being a food editor, Suki wouldn't know a good meal if one dropped from the sky into her mouth which, considering her eating disorder, would be the only way it could get in there. I tell her I'm not setting foot in another trendy gastropub. I've choked down enough charred Brussel sprouts and deconstructed hamburgers under exposed Edison bulbs to last a lifetime.

"I'll bring you something better. A real kickass column," I promise her but after I hang up I'm doubting myself. It's been a long day of nosing around the city without a scent and yet I'm already fairly stuffed.

Besides being oblivious about food, my editor doesn't know about my moonlighting either. Although it shouldn't come as a surprise. A food writer isn't that far off from a detective. Both professions are best filled by loners with impeccable memories and require eyes trained for detail. Both require keeping odd hours and low profiles—floating bogus back stories and juggling multiple aliases for reservations and credit cards, occasionally even burner phones. Both entail deploying low-key attire to keep from drawing attention or even disguises to go deep cover.

And both professions are hell on your personal life.

I pass Mandy's vegan bakery on a Highland Park street corner. She opened it a few months after ankling me. A line snakes out the door. I can smell her baking from my truck. Almond croissants, coffee cake muffins, braided cinnamon buns that leave your fingertips tacky with sweetness all day. I loved waking up to that smell filling our apartment. Even now in my truck it smells like home and I slow down, getting an eyeful of colorful clusters of hipster families giving up so much of their morning to taste her creations.

Often around last call, Xavier will wag his head at me and say I should do whatever I can to win her back. No doubt the first step would be overhauling my lifestyle. Mandy was with me a year ago when, halfway through the spiciest bowl of ramen on Sawtelle Boulevard, my nose bled and I collapsed to the tile floor, sure I was having a heart attack. An emergency room doctor that

night told me it was excesses stomach bile due to the condition called gastroesophageal reflux disease. Besides the GERDs, he clicked his pen and informed me I had low-level food poisoning and sky-high blood pressure. All this on top of my IBS, recent weight gain and cold sores when I eat eggplant or candy corn.

"You need to make some lifestyle changes," he said as my eyes met Mandy's.

"What am I supposed to do? Sit home and eat kale?"

When Mandy realized I was neither going to clean up or slow down my act, it was the Get Out of Jail card we both knew she'd been waiting for.

During those lonely last calls at the bar, I always agree with Xavier about taking action to win her back. But now I step on the gas. A perk of my new profession is I'm always on a mission with little time to wallow in our failed relationship.

My phone buzzes and I see a text from my sommelier neighbor who had been the first person I reached out to that morning. Isabelle's return text is simply a shark and thumbs up emoji. Seems promising.

Within a few blocks of driving, I get the feeling someone's following me. I recognize the boxy Subaru station wagon in need of new brake pads a few cars back. The Vulture is a little punk from the SGV trying to parlay some stellar dim sum blogging into something bigger. His real name's Zhang and he suffers from teenage acne and an over-reliance on hackneyed foodie phrases like "mouthfeel" and "fork-tender." He's tailed me in an attempt to scoop my scoops before, dashing off a quick post claiming my culinary discoveries as his own before I have time to digest and craft a decent review. He hasn't succeeded yet but it's only a matter of time.

I take it as flattery. No doubt he envies my readership as I covet his youthful bowel control.

"Not today Vulture," I mutter. "Not today."

I floor my pickup through a red light, hear the screech of brakes around me and hurtle south on Figueroa with a little toot of my horn and a middle finger out the window. The Vulture will have to upgrade from his mom's car if he ever wants to eat my

lunch.

I pull up curbside to the jazz bar in Westlake where Isabelle works, for now at least. She has a habit of berating the customers and ridiculing their palates, carrying on dueling love affairs with members of the front and back of the house, all genders. She says it's the French half of her Montreal upbringing. The plus for me is her rocky employment has yielded a fantastic array of contacts and intel on bistros and wine bars across the city.

When I arrive at the bar it's still the honeymoon phase—the hip clientele still thinks her scornful attitude is a hoot and the manager she's sleeping with looks wrapped around her finger. She waves at the customers to make room for me, gives me a heavy pour of Bordeaux and ushers over a plate of sea-salted shoestring fries and a chunk of tonight's special, a sweating hunk of porchetta oozing fennel and liver rich as fudge. I can't count on two hands how many meals I've had today.

"What would you do without me," she says.

In the past week alone, I've loaned her money, set rat traps in her apartment and dealt with a jilted ex drunkenly banging on her door at 4 am.

"You're my genie in a bottle," is all I say.

Isabelle explains she got a call from an old flame last week trying to win her back with an invitation to some kind of exotic once in a lifetime dinner thing.

"What's on the menu?"

"Omakase. You have to trust the chef and hope you don't get food poisoning." She'd turned the invite down when she heard it was in the Valley.

"But for you, I agreed to let him take me to Nobu in exchange for giving you his reservation."

She hands me a cocktail napkin with an address I don't recognize. "Tomorrow night. Dress well. Bring $1,500 in cash. Leave your phone in the car," she says, then adds: "Come over and check my rat traps this weekend."

PART III

The meal starts off normal enough. At least as normal as a $1,500 dollar a head dinner of seven strangers in a defunct ice cream shop in a strip mall with blacked-out windows deep in the Valley can be. The space is no bigger than a studio apartment with cement floors and bare bulb fixtures. A huge pink chunk of Himalayan salt sitting on the counter is the closest thing to decor. The chef, Kiro, is a graying Japanese man with a wheezing laugh and patriarchal twinkle in his eye who seems to be working all alone.

I texted Tatiana on my way that I had a lead on a journeyman chef serving an omakase menu off Van Nuys Boulevard. Since the menu was a secret, I texted her to stand by and stashed my phone in the rim of my boot. Kiro had frisked us upon entering, padding and kneading me like so much raw meat with his cold wet hands.

Standing in his tiny kitchen with us surrounding him at a makeshift sushi bar, the chef's deeply lined face is inscrutable and from his terse small talk it's hard to tell if his English is limited or he's just soft spoken. Like a croupier he deals out the first few dishes—raw oyster and poached quail egg followed by melt on your tongue sashimi and pork-filled onigiri rice balls. Between dishes, Kiro fills our glasses with sake and later whiskey, rich dessert wines and back to sake. He drinks too, but if he's getting buzzed it's impossible to tell.

"Drink, drink," he tells us. For a change, I do as I'm told.

Around a dish of creamy uni doused with caviar and yuzu juice, I feel that familiar flare-up and covertly palm a couple chalky Peptos into my mouth. I'm shoveled into my only suit for the first time since Mandy's dad died and the cheap pants already feel like they could blow any second.

"Eat, eat," he commands.

The crowd is in awe. They bow in their seats between dishes, orgasmic faces puckered around each spoonful. Everyone bookends their compliments with "chef." There's a pillow-lipped Kardashian knock-off with a young guy who looks like some kind

of prince or silent movie star. A couple bros in monogrammed cuffs speaking Mandarin. I know these types—extreme foodies that will eat anything for bragging rights.

Next to me a young Black man introduces himself as a DJ based in Miami who flew in just for this dinner after a friend attended one of the chef's underground meals in Austin last month.

"The guy's a total jazz ninja. A culinary outlaw. I hear everything after course eight is seriously *next level*," he smirks.

As if on cue, the chef dips into a metallic cooler, pulling up a long black eel like a magician's scarf and slams it on his cutting board. Less than two minutes pass between him driving a nail through its head, slicing it down the middle with his honyaki knife and thrusting tiny bowls of its squirming innards in front of us with a wink. A moment later he cracks open live lobsters with the butt of his palm, serving their carapace over tufts of crushed ice so we can pick at them as their heads are still moving. Next is octopus, sesame-oil soaked tentacles thrashing as I chew fast enough to keep the suckers from sticking to my teeth. The meal is certainly moving to, in my dining companion's words, *the next level*, but I don't excuse myself to the bathroom to text Tatiana—it's still nothing you couldn't find in a handful of smoke-filled locals-only Koreatown spots.

"Ready for soup!" Kiro declares as he doles out steaming bowls, the scalding broth splashing onto his knife-scarred hands. The other diners nudge each other conspiratorially.

"Shark fin soup, brah," the DJ giggles at me. "Next level."

Indeed, this constitutes the kind of illegal fare Tatiana tasked me to find. At least in name.

In fact, the next few dishes are basically a showcase showdown of black market specialties. "Dolphin sushi" is announced, then "kujira" before a huge platter of blubbery bites is handed family-style from patron to patron.

"We're eating Flipper and Free Willy," the DJ whispers to me through a mouthful. "It's killing me that I can't take photos!"

"Chevalier," the chef announces, and a gamey pink meat sliced nearly translucent is distributed to each us.

"Mr. Ed," the DJ says, determined to anthropomorphize

every plate. If the meal wasn't already ruined, it would be by his color commentary.

Despite my bulging stomach's protests, I eat everything and polish it off with a homemade mochi ball after which the tabs are distributed and collected, each bill folder thick with the same $1,500 in cash plus tip. Except mine.

"Hit me up on Insta. Come to a show," the DJ says on his way out the door. You bound after a meal like that.

I hand Kiro the folder with a hard look that says I know and make my way out of the shop, the last one to leave. I'll text Tatiana that this was a false alarm and call the cops myself on this fraudster. Then straight home to the bathroom as my belly is on fire and I'm out of my little pink pals.

"Stay," he asks. "One last sake."

Curious, I hang back, watching the envious gawks of the other diners as the door swings shut between us. Just the two of us, the chef slaps up the counter for me to enter the kitchen and thrusts a cup of sake in my hand. He holds his up to toast but I don't.

I'm about to call his bluff and remind him that omakase derives from the Japanese word for "entrust" when a large Latino in a black jumpsuit and glistening manbun rushes in the back door. The chef spins around in time for the man to crack him in the forehead with the butt of a .45 like he was hammering a nail. The chef sinks to his knees, stunned but conscious, and now the gun is trained on me, standing there with my sake.

It happens so fast the back door hasn't even had time to close when it opens again for a glamorous woman in enormous sunglasses and a leather duster who looks more non-plussed to see me than the chef on his knees, bleeding. She coolly side-steps a wriggling eel on the tile floor that's escaped out of an overturned cooler. My spastic colon churns into overdrive.

I'm so focused on the gun's muzzle it takes me a moment to recognize this is Tatiana, my employer.

She no longer reminds me of my ex.

"You're still here?" she sounds inconvenienced.

"Why did you come? Did you follow me? Track my phone?" My suddenly high reedy voice asking all these questions doesn't

make me sound like much of a detective, but it feels like Tatiana and I have reached the end of our professional relationship.

The only thing I know for sure right now is this woman in leather boots is not an environmentalist with a warm fuzzy for all creatures great and small. And I'm desperate for a bathroom.

"This man stole from us." She motions to the chef without looking at him. "Hijacked a whole truck for his extravagant little dinners here."

"And I led you to him."

"Good job, Mr. Mustard," she says. "You can go now. You were never here."

The muscle with the manbun flicks the ball of my nose with the gun, motioning for me to get lost. There's nothing I'd rather do.

"Actually, it does concern me. You're pistol-whipping the wrong guy." I hope they don't notice the tightness in my voice. "Not that you should be pistol-whipping anyone."

Manbun is antsy. "Want me to fix them both?" he asks, her never taking his eyes of me.

Tatiana takes a beat, hand on her hip. And that's when I see her white lobster belt buckle and realize who she is.

'Truffle' Tatiana Vennman.

The same lobster logo was emblazoned on the black Tesla vanity plate of a guy who picked Isabelle up one night for a date last year. We passed each other on our building's steps, her in an off the shoulder tight knit number and smelling of fresh juniper and me with a head cold, lugging a plastic bag hot with more pleated Korean dumplings than one man has a right to.

"You're going out with Rodney Vennman?" I said not without some jealousy and nodded towards the vanity plate. "Be on your toes. Supposedly he's a real player."

"Well so am I."

She returned early, knocked on my door and we split a couple bottles of Malbec and watched old Tony Bourdain episodes.

"Men are such shit," is all she said, staring into her wine.

That rare white lobster is the ubiquitous logo of Vennman

Family Delicacies; Vennman Family Delicacies being the biggest rare food purveyor on the west coast. Need bluefin tuna or squid ink from Spain, rare French chili peppers, Iranian caviar in bulk for a wedding, banned delicacies from salmon babies to puffin heart to pig bladders to blowfish for the international crowd at your casino… call Vennman. The father Frank handles the Bay area, the shitty player son Las Vegas and the daughter Los Angeles. In a food glossy profile, I remember a photo spread of them big-game hunting on safari with their logo on their absurdly matching hunting jackets. I heard she got the nickname Truffle Tatiana after a competitor undercut the family by passing off Chinese fakes as black French truffles to one of their casino buyers. Supposedly Tatiana ordered her muscle to chip a few of the guy's teeth force-feeding him his own inferior product. I never believed that story until now.

"The chef is guilty but not of selling your goods," I say. "The big ticket items were all fake. He was passing off sturgeon for shark fin. That was moose meat, not whale. And the chevalier wasn't gamey enough to be horse, I'm guessing venison."

If the chef's heard any of this, he doesn't show it. He's leaning against the dishwasher like he's on the verge of passing out.

Tatiana gives me a little golf clap.

"Before I was broke, I got out of LA more. I tried to be a good traveler," I say by way of explanation. "One culture's beloved pet being another's delicacy and all that."

"You have quite the impressive palate," Tatiana says. "But in this case, it's to your detriment. Sorry."

Tatiana looks at manbun and nods. He clicks off the safety. I realize too late that I probably should've invested in a firearm when I started this side hustle.

"Please don't."

I wonder what kind of tribute Suki will run for me. I can imagine The Vulture coming for my job. Maybe Xavier would hang a tasteful photo up by my barstool. Who would check Isabelle's rat traps? Not much of a legacy although I like to think a few people ate a few delicious meals that they wouldn't have without my say; that's not nothing.

I think of Mandy, a smudge of flour on her cheek when she looks up from the oven to hear the news I'm gone. Will a teardrop cut through the flour or will she just utter a sad sigh over the inevitable? At least she'll scratch her head and wonder for a moment when she hears I didn't keel over mid-meal from a heart attack but from a bullet in the face in a random kitchen in the Valley. If that isn't the world's smallest victory.

I should beg for my life but my mouth is dry. There's little doubt I'll shit my pants. Then manbun screams.

I look down and see the chef has used the same knife he opened the eel with to deftly slice across the big guy's stomach from nipple to waist. The top of his jumpsuit hangs like wrapping paper torn open to reveal a deep long gash gushing blood. He grapples to keep his insides from falling out. Blood rains down on the eel still writhing.

With a bloody knife in one hand and the gun in the other, the chef backs towards the door.

"Follow me and I kill you," he says to Tatiana who has inched up against the wall looking pale and shaken. He swings the gun in my direction.

"You driver."

The patriarchal twinkle in his eye from dinner is long gone. I walk towards him with shaky legs, averting my eyes from the big man groaning for an ambulance. Even an excess of myoglobin pooled around a rare steak can make me a bit queasy.

PART IV

Despite my protests that I've had too much sake, the chef orders me to point my truck east and drive. I covertly unbutton the top of my pants and comply. The knife gleams under the passing street lights, same with the gun in his lap. I could still really use a bathroom but it feels like we're in a rush.

"Someone following." He nods at the rearview as we cruise down a deserted Ventura. I know before I even look.

"The Vulture."

"Who?"

"It's—it's just some punk kid. He's got a dim sum blog but he's desperate to widen his readership."

"What?" He's confused. I don't blame him. It's madness what we spend our days pursuing.

Kiro is fully pivoted in his seat, clasping the gun.

"He's just a dumb foodie kid!"

"Lose him," he says. "Or I'll end him."

I accelerate till the cab of the pickup shakes and don't let up until we're on the 10 Freeway. I'm almost sad to see his shitbox recede in the rearview. He has no idea how close he came to getting his mom's tires shot out, or worse, in pursuit of a hot food post. Kid should be in bed anyway. I know I wish I was.

Kiro's chain-smoking, busy texting on his phone and clearly doesn't want to chat, but when the city's disjointed skyline is far in the rearview, I'm compelled to bring up the obvious.

"Once they poke around the kitchen, they'll understand you didn't jack their truck," I say. "So why run?"

The chef looks my way for the first time. Passing under a street light, I see he's staring at me with scorn, waiting for me to figure it out. Another mile or two goes by.

"Venmann Foods *is* counterfeit?" I venture.

"Bingo." Kiro goes back to texting on his phone. "I surprised too."

"That's why they wanted to find out who jacked their truck so bad."

The fact that Venmann is charging exorbitant sums for phony shark fin or whale sushi wouldn't just bring personal and financial ruin but incur the wrath of countless connected casino owners and fat cat restauranteurs who'd spent fortunes with them all these years.

"Why did you cook with their food if you knew it wasn't the real deal?"

"I'd already stole their truck," he shrugs. "A good chef makes do with what he has."

"It wasn't about the food at all, it was about you knowing their secret."

The chef gives a gruff chuckle as he texts. "And now you

know their secret too." Tatiana was right about a great palate being a liability.

The chef waves at me to pull off the highway and swing into a defunct gas station. We're in the middle of the desert. There's nothing but darkness for miles.

"You sure?" I ask him. He's clearly made arrangements with his people; whatever shadowy forces helped him jack the truck and shuttle him from city to city.

I suddenly don't want him to go. "Here?"

He kicks the door open without a second look and jumps out. The blood has dried on his forehead.

"Good luck, you need it." When I hesitate, he gives the bumper of my truck a kick like it's a stray dog following him. "Go."

I do as I'm told. I watch him glowing red, enveloped by my exhaust, growing smaller in my rearview until he's gone in the inky darkness. No doubt I should do the same.

Driving through the desert, I see manbun holding his guts standing among the passing cacti. I pass by him again and again.

I stop at the filthiest truck stop toilet in the Coachella Valley; the stall tattooed with obscene graffiti and the toilet seat chipped and discolored as a dead tooth. I stop counting after five courtesy flushes, vomit in the sink on my way out and deposit myself back behind the wheel, shaking and empty in every way.

As I approach the city an hour later, the sun is just starting to grope its way up through the marine layer.

Despite everything from a 15-course meal to almost being killed last night, my stomach growls. I've never been so ashamed at being insatiable.

It's so early not much is open.

I find myself parking in front of Mandy's bakery. The closed sign is up but I see her ten-speed chained by the kitchen door and know she's in there, baking something hearty and delicious. I want to sit on the counter and eat coffee cake fresh out of the oven and tell her everything that happened and how scared I feel.

"Jesus, Gordon," she'd say.

I stop short and stand there by the back door, close my eyes and inhale the fresh baking bread. It smells like her embrace and calms me.

I start thinking of the review I could type up about last night's meal and everything that followed. It would be a hell of a column if I live long enough to write it. I take one last deep breath, turn around and then I'm off to work again.

EVERYBODY'S FAMOUS

THE PARTY, IN A LOFT DOWNTOWN AND hosted by a dental hygienist notorious for his parties, is by all accounts a fucking success.

We mill about by the seven-layer dip, not because it's so delicious but because it's the best place to survey the crowd. We count half a dozen reality show personalities, four well-followed influencers, a frequent game show contestant, two warring epidemiologists, an often-blurbed TV critic and the lazy-eyed redhead who once gave a blowjob to a (at the time) very-of-the-moment indie rock band's bassist. The bartender looks familiar because, he informs us, he's played one in a lot of content. The DJ keeps reminding us of the time and station for his own local radio show, which he adds, is on the verge of syndication.

The daughter from our favorite late '90s sitcom is there. We didn't even know she lived in our city; we didn't even know she was not dead of an opiate overdose. There's half of the couple whose gender reveal party torched a quarter of Oregon. A self-castrated incel. A veterinarian victim of revenge porn.

A former Spiderman who almost killed the franchise. A visual artist better known for his philandering than his feces paintings is there; so is his wife who has far surpassed him with a series of high-profile suicide attempts. A grown-up dumpster baby says he saw Rami Malek's third cousin by the beer pong table.

"Who's that?" an 8-year-old skateboarding prodigy asks and we look over as a guy in a dirty undershirt unwittingly dribbles beer on himself. We don't recognize him and blame it on the dim lighting. After a brief debate, a tipsy hand model volunteers to stumble over and ask his name; which she does and then just as abruptly lurches back to report to us.

We all hesitantly admit we've never heard of him, which is curious, as it's a unique name. A couple of us simultaneously look him up on our phones and when that yields zero results, we exchange looks of embarrassment. We try different browsers and various spellings. We question the host who tries to bluff us, but under scrutiny admits she can't shed any light on the mystery guest either.

By now the same one syllable question ripples through the party. "Who? Who? Who?" Everyone casts glances over at this unknown guest lurching spastic, alone on the dance floor. Everyone wants to know, but no wants to ask him the obvious question. We pride ourselves on knowing everyone.

"This has to be some kind of prank?" a graphic designer with a well-circulated sex video says. Some people begin searching the apartment for hidden cameras while others question the three different guests with their own prank reality programs.

Then the photos start, subtly at first; guests nonchalantly snapping shots with their phones to send to friends, trying to find someone who knows this guy's deal.

He seems not to notice what's going on, not to see the party swarming around him, the pointed fingers, the bleary-eyed stares; all of which makes us even more curious.

The photo snapping grows more aggressive. An albino insurrectionist accused of being a pedophile on prime time blinds the guest with his video camera's spotlight. A couple Guinness World Record holders lurk behind the guest, shoulder-surfing him for their friends to snap photos. At one

point the mystery guest is knocked backwards by a thrice-canceled comedian with a telephoto lens. He lands on the sofa with a belch.

No one is getting any answers worth a damn to their text or phone calls; in fact people hearing word of what's going on are showing up in screeching taxis or double-parking and flooding into the party.

The loft is packed tight; it's hot and the floor trembles under our weight but nobody seems to care. Still seemingly oblivious, the mystery guest is sitting where he landed on the futon.

"Take my picture with him!" screams a music video background dancer. "Take my picture with him!"

She throws us her phone and races to the futon, but it's too late.

He's already getting his photo taken with someone, lots of photos. The lazy-eyed redhead is twisted over, her head buried in his lap and she goes to work on him. He sits there blinking at us, with his arms outstretched the length of the futon's back. We would never love him more.

IRISH GOODBYE

I RUN OUT OF EXCUSES. I TAP THE PHONE against my forehead but my mind has performance anxiety. I can't remember what lies I've burned through in the last few years with Derek. I only picked up the phone because I thought it was my agent. It's never my agent. There's a chance I may not even have an agent at this point.

The line is silent for a beat. Me, still as a mannequin in the middle of my studio apartment, not even breathing like maybe he'll forget who he called.

"Okay," I say finally and clear my throat. "When?"

"Now," he says. "I'm hungry. Meet me by the pool. Bring your suit."

He hangs up, then I sneeze twice. I have a touch of a cold and realize too late that should've been my excuse.

I administer my Neti pot in the shower, iron a white button-down, dress, pull on a lightweight blazer that's too small and drive to the Chateau for lunch. I don't Uber because I want to make sure I don't drink too much around Derek.

Two mixed drinks, four max.

147

I park on the street because I don't want to have to use his name with the valet and need an easy exit. I feed the meter for three hours and set an alarm on my phone. I leave my wallet in my car—Derek's stuck me with an outrageous bill more than once.

Four drinks, three hours and I'm out. Plus I have my head cold as an excuse and administering medication to my cat as a back-up.

Then there's the possibility Derek just won't be here at all. As my mother always says, Derek is on shaky terms with the truth. Or reality. I can't remember. When we were kids back east, he told me he was pen pals with Daisy Duke. He wrote "lifeguard" on a t-shirt and patrolled a rocky patch that passed for a beach in our neighborhood, blowing his whistle at anyone in earshot. When we were older, he claimed to get calls from the FBI for reasons he wouldn't discuss other than cupping the phone and mouthing "FBI" at me. His dog, I was often told, died in 9/11. He said he spearheaded an intervention for the drummer for Soul Asylum. Often after a waitress took our order and walked away, he'd look at me and say something like "Small world… Blowjob," leaving me to fill in the blanks.

Poolside at the Chateau Marmont is luxuriously quiet. A few limp bodies melt into deck chairs, a couple of men in European bathing suits play ping-pong, a billboard-sized Zendaya peek-a-boos above the palms frond. There's rumors they're going to turn this into a private club soon so I try to really take the scene in.

Not seeing him, I feel a sense of relief and am about to turn around.

"Buddy!"

Derek hoists his still intimidating frame out of the pool's deep end, his thick chest hair wet and dark as a pelt. He squish-squashes towards me. He's laughing and hugs me tight and drenches the front of my shirt. He acts happier to see me than I've ever been to see anyone in my life.

"Cricket!" he shouts past me.

A bikini'd sunbather jerks up as if from a coma, shedding glossy magazines like skin. She pads over, palming the dried

spittle from her face and squinting around like she just stepped out of a matinee.

"I was beginning to think you weren't real."

"I often feel the same way about myself."

"Hilarious," Derek says.

Cricket offers me a well-mannered smile and moderate hug. Her toned body seems like it's overcompensating for her sun-damaged face. A faded dancing bear tattoo over her bikini line looks like a bad bruise.

She'd blend in with a police lineup of all Derek's exes—a hair-chewing gallery of late 20-something prep school black sheep; rehab drop-outs with shared trust funds and severe daddy issues. I wonder if he meets them on a special app or what?

These type of girls are supposed to complement Derek's image of himself. He used to tell people he was a distant Kennedy and wears loafers, no socks even in the dead of winter.

"Remember how I told you about Leo. He's my oldest friend," he prods her.

"Childhood friend," I interject a little too fast with a modifier then laugh it off.

"Yeah, I know. Derek told me. Best friends forever." Cricket seems nice but apparently is not a big listener.

"Technically though—"

"I fucking love this kid!" Derek spanks my back with a wet hand. I feel like a patchwork teddy bear around him—button eyes loosening and hemorrhaging stuffing with his every act of affection.

Derek shadowboxes a passing waiter and orders us a round of mojitos that he assures me are the best in North America.

Ok, ok, I hear myself keep saying.

Childhood friends is accurate, even now in our 30's. Our parents owned a decrepit little pontoon boat together, *The Irish Goodbye!* They'd bought it at a police auction and yes, there was an exclamation point. The Goodbye inevitably puttered to a halt a couple gin n' tonics into any voyage leaving our mothers to play Go Fish while our fathers swam around, poking at the jammed motor with the same screwdriver that doubled as a

bottle opener. For the adults there was no rush until the liquor ran out. For me, seasick and sweaty with coconut sunscreen melting into my eyes, the rust bucket was as nauseating as any carnival ride. Derek didn't get seasick but he had his own reasons for hating the boat. He'd lean close, oblivious to my stomach-clutching, and bemoan the head-turning raspy sputter of the engine, cigarette-burned cushions and fact that this little tub didn't even have the horsepower to waterski off it. Derek had expensive taste for a grade-schooler.

He only waved at the occupants of bigger boats (which was almost everybody) and claimed to be close personal friends with the people who lived in any beachfront mansions we happened to putter past. He offered to take me to their cocktail parties and orgies. Derek was always generously inviting me to his fabricated plans. I remember him checking his cherry red Swatch and screaming at his parents something about having dinner reservations. He would offer to swim into shore and bribe the Coast Guard for a tow. He would increasingly, as his parents would say, "act up." Decorum would break down to the point where he would dance the "Disco Duck" on the bow to try to calm down, nearly hyperventilating, decrying that he had places to be. By this point the sun would be dipping and mosquitoes circling, a chill causing goosebumps. The booze would be gone and his dad would twist Derek's ear red to shut him the fuck up with his crazy stories or else.

A couple years later my parents made a stab at sobriety and started seeing Derek's parents less and gifting me a reprieve from our arranged friendship. By the time they were off the wagon again, Derek had been sent to a military academy in Michigan after threatening one of our classmates with a knife and stealing his new Schwinn ten-speed. I wasn't too broken up by the fact that we had almost no contact for years except for some long rambling letter in which he claimed it was a spoon.

Per his directions, I've brought my trunks—mesh running shorts actually. I shake off my best chinos to reveal them and follow Derek and Cricket into the pool. A swim, a light lunch, four drinks max, or was it five, and then Irish goodbye. Derek

has the personality of a rusty bear trap. In the pool, he's talking about whether we should go out to sushi or order room service for dinner.

"I rented bungalow number three through the winter." He jerks a thumb behind him. "I only wanted it for the fall but if you rent a Chateau bungalow for more than six months you get tickets to the Academy Awards so I was like fuck it."

"Hold it. I thought you were living in Nevada. You live here, in LA, now?"

"I mean can you imagine me, little Derek Fitzpatrick, at the Oscars. Insane, right."

"Don't forget about me!" Cricket pipes in as she clumsily backstrokes by us.

"You'll have to fight it out with Leo for the other ticket," Derek laughs and elbows me under water. "We'll grease you two up and have you wrestle it out."

Cricket spits a stream of chlorinated blue water through her teeth in my direction.

"Hungry?" Derek flags a waiter and orders three ostrich burgers. He says he brought the meat down with him from Carson City for me to taste—he invested in an ostrich farm. It's a side project to his tech firm. But his real passion project is the film production company he's cofounding with backers in China.

"Really?" It's easier to just pretend I believe him. "Sounds good."

"I don't know anything about movies—except every single line in *Die Hard*."

I flash to long lazy afternoons sprawled on the cool shag carpeted basement of Dereck's ranch house watching HBO and eating peanut butter and Fluff sandwiches. We could mute our favorite likes *Beverly Hills Cop, First Blood* or *Lethal Weapon* and act out all the dialogue verbatim. I'd forgotten all about that basement. It's so hard to shake certain people from your past because they hold your good memories like ransom.

"The only thing you need to know about the movies is that they're pretty much dead," I tell him.

"I love how you never kiss my ass. That's why I need you."

"Do you though?"

"Jackie Chan is having pre-dinner drinks with us later. He has an idea. Maybe you can write it. You're so much better than that but maybe you could, you know, slum it."

There's always so many questions to ask with Derek that I never bother starting. I don't tell him my parking meter will run out long before he backpeddles his way out of this Jackie Chan story.

"You're a great writer," he continues.

"He's always saying that," Cricket seconds. "You look like a writer too. With the glasses and everything. Like my high school English teacher we all had a crush on."

"He's like Bukowski meets, I dunno…. Hemingway. I still remember this story he wrote when we were kids. About a Guinea pig who turns vigilante. Little AK-47 and everything." He mimes spraying the patio of sunbathers with machine gun fire. "Hey, how the fuck is that not a movie?"

I turn and sneeze into a monogrammed hotel towel.

"You should be running this town. Every time I watch some shitty movie on a flight, I think of you and how much better your ideas are!"

"It's all about IP now," I half-heartedly defend my lackluster track record. "Rights to board games, breakfast cereals, mobile apps."

Not listening, Derek keeps talking about his film deal with China. He says Los Angeles is now an ancillary market and this deal has the potential to pay out stupid-money on a minimal investment. He's talking loud enough for a couple poolside loungers to hear.

"I want to invest." Cricket dog-paddles around us.

"No way. Save your money. Too risky business, Tom Cruise."

"But I want to."

"Forget it. Buy-in's too rich for your blood anyway."

Before she can pout, Derek pulls her to his chest for a wet splashy kiss.

Cricket seems a notch above his usual. I developed a soft spot for her when she said I looked like a writer. Or maybe it was when her butterfly stroke swept her chest clear across my back.

I wonder if she knows he did time. He still explains it away as some kind of clerical error. He once sent me a postcard from prison of a topless girl drinking a Bud on a tropical beach that said "Wish You Were Beer."

We eat our ostrich burgers and steak fries on the edge of the pool, washing it down with minty cocktails. Derek and Cricket double-team the story of their meet-cute. He was in Tulum last winter on a business retreat and she was teaching a mindfulness class at his resort. At one point during the class she told everyone to close their eyes to envision their ideal future. He left his open and so did she.

"That's when I knew it was on like Chaka Khan!" Derek gropes her and my burger is splashed with pool water.

"You know what this lunch needs," Derek announces. "Some mezcal!"

Derek tells me he's invented his own craft mezcal with the help of his degree in bio-chemistry. He says it the has highest alcohol content of any liquor in the U.S. and there's one "beta-test" bottle left in the bungalow.

"You gotta try it," he insists over my protests. "It'd be great if you could work it into the script for the Jackie Chan project too."

"Seriously though. I'm good."

"Babe, will you get it so Leo can try some with his burger." Derek asks her. "I don't trust the bellhops with the secret recipe."

Cricket obliges. She hurries out of the pool, tosses on her terrycloth robe and lets the belt trail behind her. I feel bad making her run an errand and offer to go along. Plus, I need a sobering time-out away from Derek. It's been two and half hours, nearly five drinks already.

"I have to use the bathroom anyway," I say to Derek, grabbing my button-down and following her down a leafy path.

"Don't clog it!" Derek yells across the patio and laughs.

The understated bungalow is filled with midcentury furnishings and natural light, tasteful and retro. It's not the one where John Belushi died but Cricket says that's close by. This place for a month surely costs more than I made last year.

I pour a glass of water from the tap and can hear Cricket

riffling through Derek's suitcase in the master bedroom.

"Bingo!" Cricket meets me in the living room with the mezcal, her robe still hanging open. The bottle is tall and ornate, full of a jaundiced substance hiding behind a peeling label with a black and white photo of a shirtless Derek squinting into the barren desert and looking too big for the donkey he's straddling. The heavily flaming font reads Derek's Hombre Fuerte Small Batch Mezcal.

Cricket informs me straight-faced that Derek has already sold 100,000 units of this to Whole Foods for the fall.

"Really? He's a real Renaissance man."

"He certainly is."

We exchange an awkward smile. I finish my water. I definitely can't have another cocktail or choke down any mezcal at the pool without abandoning my plan.

She's a nice girl and I feel like I owe her something.

"The movie business is pretty risky."

"That's Derek. He never thinks small."

"Derek sometimes tells tall tales is what I'm saying."

"So does Elon Musk, right."

"I guess. Maybe though Derek isn't as … Maybe it's better not to invest with Derek right off the bat. You know, maybe hold off…" I say, then add just to be clear. "Hold onto your money."

Cricket soaks it in. I'm half expecting her to break into tears. Instead she smiles.

"Derek told me you'd do this."

I raise my eyebrows as if to say, do what.

"He told me you didn't believe in yourself. Never had. And that you were jealous that Derek did."

"Now hold on—"

"He said things hadn't panned out for you in LA. Not by a nautical mile. But that I shouldn't hold it against you." She says it all matter of fact, like it's just so obvious anyway. "So I won't hold it against you, but you know, be a little appreciative."

"For what?"

"I mean he did just buy you lunch for one thing."

I suddenly see myself through her eyes—my writerly pretense, de facto bathing suit and starchy advice—and it's

unbearable.

She probably thinks I want to fuck her too. I go to drink my water but the glass is empty and so surprisingly light in my hand that I bang my front tooth on the rim. My math on how many drinks I've had is fuzzy. I mumble something about being glad we can be honest with each other. She says she's going to use the bathroom and I should hustle back with the bottle.

I walk back into the choppy sunlight and head towards the pool. I can hear Derek in the shallow end, he's talking about his China deal with someone with a British accent. The British accent says he too is heavily invested in China. "Who isn't?" Derek cordially invites the British voice back to his bungalow later to hear more and maybe even get in on the action.

I quicken my pace and pass right by the pool. I continue winding my way through the overgrown narrow pathways towards the stately valet station and hustle past the sneering throng of unshaven paparazzi loitering by the mouth of the driveway.

Then I'm right back in the bustle of Sunset Boulevard, so ear-splitting and tacky in comparison, walking in my sopping running shorts and bare feet. I've abandoned my best chinos, summer blazer and tennis sneakers at the Chateau pool; probably not a fair trade for an artisanal bottle of nearly lethal mezcal.

I drop the bottle in the guitar case of a dreadlocked street busker playing a Sublime song outside Crazy Girls strip bar. He gives me a pitying look as I have a spastic sneezing fit into my pruned hand.

The eyes of Zendaya and countless other billboard models look down on me like so many stained-glass saints as I scuttle down the hot sidewalk. Cricket's reproach still singes my ears.

I have a ticket on my windshield. 3 hours, 4 or 5 drinks. I just missed my window.

I pluck it out from under the wiper to see the damage and spot a passing limo heading up towards the Chateau.

I see myself floating past in the stretch's black funhouse reflection, looking lost and shapeless like a drowned man. The tinted windows are rolled down just enough for me to think that could be Jackie Chan I spy back there.

Then guess what I do.

ABOUT THE AUTHOR

Duncan Birmingham is a writer and filmmaker living in Los Angeles. He's been a writer and producer on numerous TV shows including *Maron* (starring Marc Maron) and *Blunt Talk*. Short films he's written and directed have premiered at film festivals including Sundance and AFI. His stories have appeared in literary magazines including *Mystery Tribune*, *Maudlin House, nerve, Juked, 7x7, Vol. 1 Brooklyn* and *Joyland*.

Thanks to my many teachers through the years as well as friends I annoyed asking for help with titles. Special thanks to Mallory Smart, Jonathan Ames, Gina Frangello, DeWitt Henry, Tod Goldberg, Rachel Sherman, Bud Smith, Lane Kneedler aka Beef Erikson, Suzy Birmingham, Steve Dunn and the Norton Island Residency Program for Writers & Artists.

The Cult In My Garage

. An office worker hopes a new drug will remedy her toxic personal life... A food blogger moonlights as a detective to give meaning to his gluttony... A rehabbed addict proselytizes with an increasingly bizarre methodology... Lovesick strangers try to heal through a dating app that promises a unique form of catharsis... A quarantined man starts having vivid dreams he's convinced aren't his own... At a party where everyone's "somebody" the crowd grows feverishly reverential of one guest's anonymity...

In the prescient world of 'The Cult in My Garage', the characters are desperate for meaning and hungry for connection. Time and again, their attempts at betterment snowball into disaster or backfire spectacularly. And yet they still find ways to dust themselves off and salvage meaning.

THE CULT
IN MY
GARAGE

STORIES BY

DUNCAN
BIRMINGHAM

I asked my wife, 'Is there somebody else?'
She said, 'There must be.'
—Rodney Dangerfield

Early Drafts Of:

"Classic Amy" originally appeared in *Maudlin House*

"Good in a Room" originally appeared in *Joyland*

"Better Than Drugs" (as "Old Buddies")
originally appeared in *Brooklyn Vol 1*

"Quebec" originally appeared in *Juked*

"Gordon's Revenge" originally appeared in *Brooklyn Vol 1*

"The Foodie Detective" (as "The Starving Detective")
originally appeared in *Mystery Tribune*

"There Are No Hills on the Cape" originally appeared in
Joyland

"Everybody's Famous" originally appeared in *Storychord*

"Irish Goodbye" originally appeared in *Joyland*

maudlinhouse.net
twitter.com/maudlinhouse

The Cult in My Garage
Copyright © 2021 by Duncan Birmingham

TABLE OF CONTENTS

CLASSIC AMY

AMY WAS IN A MOOD. FIRST THE DJ DUMPED her over text from some full moon party in the desert before she had even washed his scent out of her sheets from the previous weekend, then her psychologist cleared his throat and dropped her mid-session. Sure, she had been flirting with him again, but still.

"I don't think this is working for me," she relayed Dr. Ted's words to her sister Gwen over lunch in Santa Monica. "Exactly the same words the DJ texted me!"

"Look," her sister started. "There's a reason I wanted to have lunch today."

"I thought it was for my birthday."

"Yes. That's a component for sure."

Just then the waitress came over to fill their water glasses and compliment Amy on the yumminess of the baby propped in a high chair between the women, gnawing a corner of the white tablecloth.

"Yummy for sure but it's hers." Amy leveled a breadstick at her sister.

"You just gave birth? No way! You look amazing."

"Hold it," Amy said through a mouthful of breadstick. "She looks amazing and I look like I just gave birth?"

"You look like… you need more iced tea," the waitress called over her shoulder, power-walking far away.

"Seriously?" Amy mimed knifing the waitress with a new breadstick. "And why am I the only one eating these breadsticks?"

"So, like I was saying you need to find someone. I'm worried you're drifting into spinster territory."

"What? You weren't saying that at all."

"Oh? Well I was delicately winding up to it."

"Maybe I'm fulfilled by my career and friendships."

"You're insanely lonely, you hate yourself and your job is shit. I'm your best friend by default."

Even for her sister this was harsh, and Amy told her as much.

"Those are your exact words." Gwen held up her phone to show Amy. "See? You texted me at 4 am Saturday night."

The baby giggled. Amy shot it a look.

"Sanjay and I met this great guy last week at a Save the Bay thing. Sanj is going to invest in his start-up. Successful, cute, new in town. His name's Doug—"

"Doug!" Amy made a sour face. "I can't come with a Doug!"

Suddenly, a cake appeared, propelled by the singing waitstaff. It was just a slice really but large enough for Amy to eat and hate herself while Gwen watched. Amy was already attempting to blow it out before the dish was even set down but there were too many freaking candles.

Gwen held her phone and announced she was live streaming.

"I hate this," Amy said.

"I know," Gwen said from behind the phone. "Here's to wishing you have someone you like better than me to spend your next birthday with."

It was the first thing she said that Amy could agree with.

ome, well-bred and earnest like a high
/ho knew how to dress or a young mayor
city who came from money. He pulled her